THE KEEPER

THE UNGUARDED STORY OF TIM HOWARD

THE KEEPER

THE UNGUARDED STORY OF TIM HOWARD

with Ali Benjamin

HARPER

An imprint of HarperCollinsPublishers

AUTHOR'S NOTE:
The game I play has a different name in the US than it does in the
rest of the world. I'm one of the few people who uses both. When
I'm playing for my club team, Everton, in Liverpool, England, I refer
to it as "football," but when I'm playing for the US National Team I
call it soccer. In this book, I have decided to go with soccer.

Some names and identifying details have been changed to protect
the privacy of individuals.

ISBN 978-0-06-238755-4 (trade bdg.)
ISBN 978-0-06-239596-2 (special edition)

14 15 16 17 18 LP/RRDH 10 9 8 7 6 5 4 3 2 1
❖
First Edition

For my mom, who gave me everything,
and for Alivia and Jacob, who are my everything

CONTENTS

PART ONE

PROLOGUE

ARENA FONTE NOVA
SALVADOR, BRAZIL
JUST BEFORE THE USA-BELGIUM WORLD CUP
GAME
July 2, 2014

EVEN FROM THE LOCKER ROOM, I CAN HEAR THE RUMBLING OF the crowd. The drumbeats. The chants: "USA! USA!"

I believe that we will win. That's the chant that our fans have been cheering at our games. It's become an anthem for us.

And I do. I believe.

I got ready for this game the way I do for every game I play. I have a lot of pregame rituals. Whether it's a "small" game—like a friendly match—or a big one, like today's World Cup game, I do things the exact same way every time. I get dressed in the same way—I put on my shin guards, socks, and shoes, right leg first, then left. I tape my fingers in the same precise pattern. I touch things— the field, the ball—in the exact same way. I warm up the same way.

It's the routine I used during my first match for Everton, the team I play for in England. Five hundred games later, the routine still works.

It might seem crazy to everyone else, but to me, it makes all the sense in the world. It's the best way I know to feel calm and in control.

After all, I can't know what's coming during a game. I only know how to get myself into a place where I feel ready for it.

Our coach, Jürgen Klinsmann, moves through the locker room. He's friendly. Upbeat. He claps players on the back, speaking to them one at a time.

Near me, Clint Dempsey pulls his yellow captain's armband over his bicep. His hardened jawline, his steely eyes, tell me all I need to know: it's on.

There's a poster on the wall of the locker room. It's a close-up image of a bald eagle staring straight ahead. The words next to it:

WE CAN AND WE WILL.
ONE NATION, ONE TEAM.

Something is in the air. I can feel it.

I believe that we will win.

I believe that we have everything we need this time.

We are strong. We have speed and power and grit.

We've been beating powerhouse countries for over a decade.

We've surprised the soccer world again and again and again.

Last night, my teammate Michael Bradley looked me straight in the eye and said the thing that everyone seems to be feeling, but that no one had yet said out loud: "I really think we can do this. I really think we can win tomorrow."

I believe that we will win.

Clint Dempsey calls us over. "Let's get this done for our country, okay?"

Everyone nods. We're pumped now. "Okay then. Let's bring it in on three."

We place our hands in a circle. Dempsey counts, and we respond in unison. *"USA!"*

We walk out of the locker room. In the hallway, I recognize two of my Everton teammates: Kevin Mirallas and Romelu Lukaku. They are Belgian, so we're not teammates today. We're opponents. We hug, but we all feel the tension.

Belgium's starters line up; we fall into place beside

them, our eyes fixed straight ahead.

The referee stands between us, holding the ball.

I ask the ref if I can hold it. Another ritual. I turn it over in my hands, feeling its curve against my keeper's gloves.

Then I make the sign of the cross.

Michael bellows, "Come on, boys!"

Almost there.

That's when I say the same prayer I always do just before a game, the one for my children: I pray that they'll know how much I love them, that they'll be protected from harm. Saying these words—the ones I always say—puts everything in perspective for me. It grounds me.

We walk out of the tunnel, and the stadium erupts.

It's all color and light. The green of the field, the ref's neon jersey, the blue stands that surround us. Flags and scarves and banners everywhere, in red, white, and blue.

It's still daytime, but the floodlights are on. When the game is over, it will be nighttime. Everything that's about to happen will already be fading into the past.

When I reach the field, it's time to bend down and touch the grass. Then I make the sign of the cross again. Two more rituals.

I believe that we will win.

Somewhere in that roaring crowd sits my mom. Just knowing she's there gives me the old feeling I had as a kid playing recreational soccer. Back then, if I had a rough patch in a game, she moved closer to me. Her presence gave me strength. It's like she was saying, *You'll be okay, Tim.*

I still feel that message right now.

I know others are watching back in the States, too. My old coach. My dad. My kids. My brother. Some of the guys I played with through the years.

And so many more. Nearly twenty-five million people in the United States watched our last game—far more than had tuned into either the World Series or the NBA finals. At this very moment, people are crowded into public spaces all over the United States, watching together. Twenty-eight thousand in Chicago's Soldier Field. Twenty thousand in Dallas. Ten thousand in the small city of Bethlehem, Pennsylvania.

They're out there now, wearing Uncle Sam hats, Stars and Stripes T-shirts, their faces painted red, white, and blue. They're out there for us.

I believe that we will win.

When the whistle blows, I cross myself for the third time. The final ritual.

We can do this. I am certain of it. We can win today. And if we do, if we advance to the quarterfinals, it will be the greatest thing I've ever done for my country.

This is going to be the game of my life.

CHAPTER 1
IN NEW JERSEY, ANYTHING IS POSSIBLE

I WAS BORN ON MARCH 16, 1979, AND RAISED IN NEW JERSEY.
That's where my goalkeeping got started.

I spent my childhood following my older brother, Chris, around Northwood Estates, our apartment complex in North Brunswick. "Northwood Estates" sounds fancy—like it might be filled with rolling hills and English gardens. Actually, these were plain apartment buildings, wedged between two highways, a short distance from a pizza parlor and not much else.

We didn't have much. My mother raised me and Chris in a small, one-bedroom apartment—my "bedroom" was supposed to be the dining room, and my brother's room was in the basement. Mom worked long hours in an office that was over an hour's drive in each direction. She didn't earn much. She had to scrimp and save to pay for food and rent.

I had friends who had far more than I did. They lived in bigger homes in a development called Fox Hill Run. I was always astonished when I visited them. Their homes had high ceilings and white carpets and light streaming in through skylights. They had pool tables in finished basements, huge backyards with pools, and gazebos where their parents entertained.

If you could make it to Fox Hill Run, I thought, you really had it made.

But if Jersey gave me anything, it gave me a sense of perspective. A few miles in the other direction lay a rough apartment complex, which had a reputation for gang violence and drugs.

We heard many different languages in Northwood Estates: Spanish, Polish, Punjabi, Italian, Hebrew. Leaving our apartment each day, we were often hit with a mysterious odor; it took years before my brother and I figured out that it was the smell of bubbling curry, the nightly fare for a Sikh family who lived in an adjoining building. One of the kids in that family, Jagjit, rode his bike with us, occasionally stopping to adjust his turban.

* * *

That apartment complex was a melting pot of cultures and skin colors. In that way, Chris and I fit right in.

My father was black, a truck driver, who moved out when I was still a toddler. My mother was white, born in Hungary. Mom's mom was a teacher, and her dad was a former Hungarian prisoner of war. The world around me was filled with so many different kinds of people—so many shades of skin color—that I never bothered to wonder about my own skin until I was ten years old.

"Why does your skin have that dark color?" a white classmate asked one afternoon.

I looked at my arm and considered his question. My skin *was* pretty dark, now that he mentioned it. I shrugged.

"My family went to Florida," I said. It was true. We had been to Florida . . . about twenty weeks before. "I guess I still have a tan."

Mom worried about money constantly. "Turn off the lights!" she always hollered at us as Chris and I tumbled from room to room, wrestling and smacking each other in the head. "You're wasting energy!"

She clipped coupons before our weekly trips to the grocery store, and then filled the cart with generic-brand boxes of food. For housewares, we shopped at the US1 Flea Market, where we'd find garage-sale prices. For clothes,

it was always Sears; the knees on their pants were rein-
forced with double the fabric, so they lasted longer.

On winter mornings, we woke up shivering. Then we
walked into our tiny kitchen. There, Mom turned on all
four burners on the stove, and we'd huddle around it to
get warm.

Mom's long hours at work meant that Chris and I
spent a lot of time alone . . . especially in the afternoons,
after we stepped off the school bus.

In Northwood Estates, we could always find a game
being played somewhere—street hockey or touch football or manhunt in the woods. Chris and I dashed over
to the basketball hoop to play some pickup, or headed to
the scrubby field to hit a baseball. Sometimes we'd toss
footballs while dodging cars in the parking lot.

I wanted to play everything.

I wanted to *win* everything.

Most of the kids organizing the games were years
older than I was. They were bigger and tougher. They
had far more skills.

I didn't care, though. I wanted to be as good as they
were—*better* than they were.

I jumped in and played hard, no matter how much I
got knocked around. And boy, did I get knocked around.

Once, on the basketball court, a kid named Jimmy
fouled me so hard I dropped to the ground. Jimmy was

three years older than I was. He was a terrific basketball player . . . and he was tough as nails. Once, I'd seen Jimmy get into a fistfight with another player—a fight so rough that Jimmy had started bleeding from the eye and lip. When the fight broke up, Jimmy returned to the game, still bleeding, as if nothing had happened.

Now from the ground, I looked up at Jimmy. He stared back at me, unblinking. It was as if he was saying, *I don't care how old you are. I'm not going to let you win this game.*

I met Jimmy's stare. *Well, I'm not going to let you win just because you knocked me down.*

I got up. He tossed me the ball, hard, and we started playing again.

If things got too rough, though, my brother was right there for me. Chris might have punched me regularly around the house—often delivering a blow to the gut so hard it knocked the wind out of me—but he was always the first to defend me. Chris was fearless. During another basketball game—I remember Chris was on crutches at the time, just watching me play—I got into a scuffle with a wild kid named Darren. Darren hit me, and in an instant, Chris was off his crutches, punching the daylights out of him.

He hit Darren with such force that we'd later learn he had broken Darren's nose.

That night, though, Chris punched me in the gut. "I saved your butt, jerk." I hit him back, lightly, but it was enough.

Then I ran like crazy, knocking over lamps and books as I barreled through the apartment.

Mom begged us to "Please, for goodness' sake, settle down."

Just business as usual for the Howard boys.

Each night when Mom got home from work, she set her purse down and headed straight for the kitchen to scrape together some sort of dinner for us. By this point, Chris and I were as hungry as bears. We'd eat everything she put in front of us: hot dogs, mac and cheese, cans of beans, with bowls of cereal to finish it off.

After dinner, we'd be at it again. We wrestled and rolled around on the carpet. We were both big kids, all limbs and elbows and energy. We did a lot of damage when we got brawling.

My mom was overworked and overtired by that point. All she wanted was to put a record on, hear a few bars of her favorite music—mellow music, like Joan Baez or Chuck Mangione. She wanted to close her eyes for a few minutes before she did the dishes—just a few minutes of peace. She'd beg us to please, *please* be just a little quieter.

When we weren't, she finally broke. She started shouting in Hungarian, her native language—throaty curses that neither Chris nor I understood. To us, her words sounded like sheer gibberish. And although she was steaming by now, ready to toss us out of the apartment window, we couldn't help ourselves: we'd start laughing at all Mom's crazy sounds.

"Enough," she'd say, fire in her eyes. "Downstairs." She'd chase us out of the kitchen and out of the living room, down to the basement, to Chris's makeshift bedroom. There, we'd fall to the floor holding our stomachs. We were laughing that hard.

Thursdays were spent with Poppa and Momma—my mom's parents—in their split-level home in the nearby town of East Brunswick. Poppa had this crazy trick: he could fall asleep in an instant.

"I'm going to take a nap now," he'd announce. "Ten minutes." Then, wherever he was sitting—the kitchen table, the sofa—he'd shut his eyes. Seconds later, he'd be conked out, his chest rising and falling in the deep, slow rhythm of a person at rest.

"Poppa?" Chris would say. Then he'd say it louder. "Poppa?"

Poppa might let out a snore then, a single throaty rumble. But he wouldn't wake up until the ten minutes were up—exactly ten minutes.

Poppa picked up that trick while he was a prisoner during World War II in Hungary, in 1944–45. He and his fellow prisoners learned to sleep as they marched, or to catch sleep in whatever tiny moments they had.

After the war, Poppa worked on factory floors for eleven years. Then, in 1956, there was an uprising against the Communist government that had been in power since the war. Poppa had helped organize factory workers during the uprising. Eventually, he was informed he was to be tried for treason—a certain death sentence. So Momma and Poppa escaped from Hungary in the middle of the night, with my mother, then six, and her infant brother, Akos, in tow.

Poppa would tell us these stories as Momma bustled around the kitchen preparing stuffed cabbage and dumplings and meat dishes heavy with paprika. As the food bubbled on the stove, my brother and I listened, completely rapt, to Poppa's thickly accented tales.

When Poppa had arrived in New Jersey with his family, they had nothing whatsoever—no home, no money, no friends. He found a job as a factory janitor at Johnson & Johnson, and over the next three decades, he slowly worked his way up through the ranks of the company. By the time he retired, he'd become a senior research scientist. He'd even filed a number of patents in his name!

This house we sat in every Thursday, with its tidy lawn and middle-class comforts, was a testament to Poppa's success in America. It was proof that freedom and hard work made everything possible.

My Nana, my father's mom, lived in a rough neighborhood.

When I visited her, the air always seemed filled with danger and the threat of crime.

Nana had been a single mom with five children. Somehow she'd raised them all on cafeteria wages—she served meals in the dining hall at Rutgers University.

Nana's kids stayed near to her when they grew up. Then they had their own kids, so I had lots of cousins nearby. My cousins and I met up at Nana's—sometimes fifteen of us all at once. We'd run around screaming and shouting at one another, slamming doors as we tore around her apartment. When the chaos got to be too much for her, Nana would call out, "Where's my switch? I'm getting my switch." Then she'd open the back door and snap off a branch from a scrubby bush growing just outside her door. She pulled off the leaves and started waving the thing around. If we didn't move fast, she'd hit the back of our legs with that branch. We'd burst out of the house, running for our lives, this huge caravan of

kids all scared to death of the strongest, toughest grand-
mother imaginable.

That was my childhood in New Jersey: Sikh immigrants
and the sprawling lawns of Fox Hill Run. Hungarian
paprikash and scrappy games of pickup basketball. The
force of Jimmy's fist, and the sting of Nana's switch. Coupons and flea markets. The idea that you could start a
new life as a janitor and work your way into the middle
class.

New Jersey was promise. New Jersey was the American Dream. New Jersey was the world, and the world
could be mine for the taking. All I had to do was show up,
day after day, give it everything I had, and keep the faith.

It was in New Jersey that I first understood this: anything is possible.

CHAPTER 2
GOALS THAT MATTERED

If only you'd apply yourself, Tim . . .
You're a good kid, but you lack ambition.
If only you worked as hard in the classroom as you do
at sports . . .

I WAS NOT A GOOD STUDENT. I COULDN'T SIT STILL, COULDN'T
focus. I wanted to be anywhere but school.

My mom always said when I was a baby, it was like
all my senses were turned on high alert. I hated the feel
of cool air on my skin, so I screamed every time I was
changed. I hollered when I was bathed. The water was
either too warm, or too cool. I didn't sleep through the

night until I was seven years old. Mom spent hours getting me to sleep each night—she played music, stroked my face, tried to help me relax enough to close my eyes. When I finally did, she tiptoed out of the room, praying that I'd stay asleep. Twenty minutes later, though, if a floorboard creaked, or a faraway police siren sounded, my eyes popped open all over again.

I was terrified of heights. I startled easily. I was acutely affected by even slight changes in light and sound and sensation.

I was just very, very sensitive to the environment around me. And by the time I got older, the classroom felt like the worst place of all. When I was in school, I couldn't stop focusing on things like the *tick tick* of the clock on the wall, or the hum of the fluorescent lights overhead. The screech of chairs scraping across floors, the hardness of the seat beneath me.

And worse: there were all those long, long hours of sitting still.

I couldn't understand how other kids sat there. They tolerated school, like it didn't even bother them.

For me, it was unbearable.

I escaped the only way I knew how: I became the kid who raised his hand five, six, seven times a day, asking to go to the bathroom. Sometimes I'd say I needed to go see the school nurse. I wasn't actually sick. It was just that anywhere, even the nurse's office, was better than being stuck at my desk. I'm pretty sure that the first record I ever set was Boy Most Likely to Be Out of the Classroom—and I wasn't even in second grade yet.

"Oh, Tim," my teachers would sigh when I squirmed in my seat or was unable to answer a question. "If you'd only pay attention . . ."

But to me, the days at the Arthur M. Judd Elementary School were just something to be endured. They were the things I had to do until I could burst into the wide-open air and get to the things that really mattered: sports.

When I was six, my mom signed me up for sports leagues. First, she signed me up for T-ball. Because I was a big kid, standing head and shoulders above all the other kids my age, the coach put me in the outfield.

But nothing happened in the outfield. I'd stand there and wait as a bunch of short kids swung and missed. So as I stood around in the field, I'd make up a game in my head and catch imaginary drives. Mom says I acted like a sports commentator for whatever game played in my mind. *And he hits the ball into the outfield . . . and the outfielders are running to get it . . . he's rounding third base and the crowd goes wild. . . .*

By the time the other team had gotten three outs, I was running like crazy all over that outfield. I was waving my arms and calling imaginary action into the air.

Then we tried recreational soccer. My first team was called the Rangers, and we wore green T-shirts.

I couldn't dribble or trap a ball or even complete a pass to a teammate. But I was fast. I ran past the other players, got to the ball first, and kicked it far up the field.

During one early game, I remember the dad of one of the opposing players kept shouting to his son, "Get that jolly green giant! Don't let the jolly green giant get the ball!"

He was talking about me, of course, the tall kid in the green shirt. I looked over at the edge of the field and met my mom's eye. I could tell she was as bothered by that man as I was. But she nodded at me reassuringly. *It's okay, Tim,* she seemed to be saying. *You just keep playing.*

Mostly, though, I loved everything about playing soccer. I loved smelling the grass on the field and lacing up my cleats before practice. I loved the nylon uniforms and the splotches of mud that appeared on my legs after practicing in the rain.

I cried when games were rained out. While some kids faked being sick to get out of practice, I would sometimes fake being well when I *was* really sick so I wouldn't miss anything.

Most of all, I loved sliding, almost like a baseball player, to get to the ball.

Or sometimes I would miss the ball and slide into my opponent's legs.

After a few too many slides, my coach scolded me. "Just run and kick the ball the way everyone else does."

I tried to do what he said, but I couldn't help myself: I loved the way sliding intimidated my opponents. I loved how it made them step back warily. I loved the feeling of the slide itself.

Sliding is a big goalkeeper's move. It was like there was already a goalkeeper in me, trying to get out.

Because I was tall, and relatively fearless, the coach of the Rangers wanted me in goal.

But I didn't like standing in goal. Standing in goal was as bad as standing in the outfield in T-ball. It wasn't where the action was.

If I was standing in goal, I couldn't score.

Playing up front, I was always just one goal away from being a hero. As a goalie, I was always one goal away from being a villain.

"If you play goalie for half the game," Coach pleaded with me, "I'll let you be the striker for the other half."

I sighed and did as I was told, but I didn't like it.

I watched and waited for the action to come toward me.

Then, suddenly, the other team started racing down the field. They'd kick, and the ball would sail right at me. At that moment, I felt the weight of the whole team—which, as a kid, meant the expectations of the whole world—squarely on me.

I wanted so badly to stop the ball. At the same time, I was terrified I wouldn't.

Often I did stop it. But when I didn't—and when the other team's parents started cheering and the kids who weren't in green started leaping all over the field—I felt ashamed.

It was too much. I'd start crying right there on the field.

That's when I'd see my mom get up. She'd shift her chair a little closer to where I stood. Then she'd meet my eye.

It's okay, Tim, she told me again with her look. *You'll be okay.*

Just seeing her there was enough to make me feel better.

I'd take one deep breath and get back in the game.

CHAPTER 3
TOUCHES AND TICS

I WAS TEN WHEN THE SYMPTOMS BEGAN TO APPEAR.

First came the touching: I walked through the house tapping certain objects in a particular order, with a specific rhythm. *Touch the railing. Touch the doorframe. Touch the light switch. Touch the wall. Touch the picture.*

The pattern might vary, but there was always a pattern, and it had to be followed. If it wasn't—if I tried to resist, or if Chris knocked into me at the wrong time—I'd have to start all over again.

It didn't matter if I was starving and dinner was on the table. It didn't matter how badly I needed to go to the

bathroom. The pattern inside my head was more important than the reality on the outside. I had to obey. I *had*
to touch these things, and in exactly the right order; it
was urgent.

One part of my brain, the logical part, understood
that these rituals made no sense, that nothing bad would
happen if I didn't practice them. But knowing that only
made things worse. If it didn't make sense, then why
couldn't I stop?

What was wrong with me?

Then it started happening outside the house, on my way
to school. Each day, I walked to Judd carrying a schoolbag full of books.

I'd spot things along the way—a rock, for example.
There was nothing special about the rock's shape or
texture or color; it looked like every other rock. But suddenly, that rock mattered. It was the most important
object in the world.

Pick up that rock, my mind commanded. *You'd better
pick up that rock.*

I'd try so hard not to. I'd grit my teeth and stare
ahead. I might manage to walk a few steps before my
heart started pounding.

Go back, my body urged me. *Pick up that rock.*

If I resisted, I'd start to panic. My stomach churned.

I might break out into a sweat. I'd start to breathe harder, like I'd been running.

It felt like the fate of the universe rested on this one act: picking up that stupid rock.

Finally, I'd give in, turn around, get the rock, and drop it into my bag. When I did, I felt great relief.

Everything was okay. The universe was back in control again.

Over the following weeks, my schoolbag became filled with rocks and acorns and dirt and flowers and grass stems—all this weird stuff I picked up on the way to school. As I got closer to school, I smiled and waved at the crossing guard, as if everything was perfectly fine. As if I hadn't just lost a battle with my own brain.

As if I didn't feel urges to do things I could never in a million years understand.

Next came the tics.

Tics are motions or sounds that are difficult to control. And boy, did I make motions and sounds.

I started blinking—not like ordinary blinks. These were forceful, deliberate blinks that I couldn't stop.

Then I began to clear my throat over and over.

Then there were facial jerks. Shoulder shrugs. Eye rolling.

With each tic, I felt the urge welling up. If I tried

not to have the tic, I'd feel great stress building up—the same kind of stress I felt when I didn't pick up the rock, or touch things in the right pattern.

Then, as soon as I had the tic—as soon as I cleared my throat or shrugged my shoulder—I'd feel normal again. But just for a short while. Seconds later, the cycle would start all over again: Urge. Stress. Tic. Relief.

I tried to force myself *not* to tic. But these tics were like breathing for me—I might be able to stop for a while, but I just couldn't stop forever.

In school, teachers snapped at me in class—*Sit still. Stop clearing your throat.*

Other kids laughed. *What's going on with your face?*

At home, Mom stayed quiet, but I felt her watching me. I saw how her eyes flicked to whatever part of my body I'd just moved.

When she noticed, her face showed the same concern she had when she realized Chris and I had outgrown our winter coats and needed new ones. It was the same look she wore whenever she opened bills.

I could tell it worried her a lot.

I hated that I was adding to her concerns. I hated that I couldn't just stop these weird movements.

But of course, that was impossible. If I *didn't* do these things, if I tried to act like everyone else, everything in my life felt wrong.

Not just wrong. Awful. Like the whole world was about to end.

On the soccer field, though, I felt better. More in control.

When the action was on the other end of the field, I still had tics. But the nearer the action came to me, the more in control I felt.

By the time it was moving toward me—poof!—all those thoughts and urges disappeared.

Standing in goal, I would kick the ball, or catch it, or parry it. Or it would fly past me, and I'd have to pick it out of the net while the other team celebrated.

Either way, whether I had succeeded or failed, that's when everything came back again.

Touch the ground. Touch the post. Twitch, jerk, cough.

When I was eleven, I developed a new symptom, the worst one yet: I had to touch people before I talked to them. When I say "had to," that's exactly what I mean: if I didn't touch them first, I couldn't speak.

It was like touching the person opened the door to my thoughts, allowed ideas to flow into words. But if I didn't touch the person, that door remained stubbornly shut. Everything just kept thumping against the inside of my brain, unable to escape.

At school, I tried to hide this tic through casual touches. Sometimes I'd punch a kid lightly in the arm before speaking. Or I'd tap a friend on the opposite shoulder from behind, as if trying to make them look the wrong way. Sometimes I'd fake bumping into them.

At home, I'd touch my mom on the shoulder. One tap. Then I could talk.

She glanced down at the place I'd just touched. She didn't say a word.

After a while, when I stepped toward her, she began stepping backward, just out of reach.

"Go ahead," she encouraged. "What were you saying?"

But I couldn't tell her. I stood there mute, mouth hanging open. *Just tell her,* my brain screamed. *Tell her something.*

No words came. I was helpless—yet again—to control my own brain, my own body.

Mom took me to a doctor. He asked us lots of questions about my behavior. Mom described it all: the compulsive touching, the twitching, the blinking. I might have thought I was hiding them successfully. I hadn't been. It turns out Mom had noticed everything.

The doctor diagnosed me with two conditions.

First, I had obsessive-compulsive disorder. OCD is

an anxiety disorder whose main symptoms are unwelcome and irrational thoughts. There are many different ways these thoughts can present themselves; in my case, the thoughts were things like, *Touch the banister. Pick up that rock. You'd better do it or something terrible will happen.*

Second, I had Tourette Syndrome, TS. It creates motor and vocal urges.

TS has a funny reputation out in the world. Most people think of it as a "cursing disease," a disorder that makes people say bad words uncontrollably. That form does exist—there are, in fact, people with TS who cannot help cursing. But that form is rare. Most tics are more like the ones that I had. Some people hoot, some cough, some hiss or bark or grunt. They might wrinkle their nose or kick or grimace. Sometimes, other people barely notice tics, but sometimes tics are so huge, people can't help but notice.

The doctor said my case was "mild"—though it didn't feel mild to me.

As we walked out of the office, he said, almost as an afterthought, "Mrs. Howard?"

Mom turned around.

"I've been doing this a long time," he said. "And there's one thing I'm absolutely sure of: with every challenge a kid faces, there's some flip side."

"Like what?"

"Well, it depends on the person," he answered. "But I've noticed a lot of kids with OCD and TS are really good at hyperfocusing—at staying with a task until they've perfected it."

Mom listened.

"Anyhow," the doctor said, "I really do believe that there's always a flip side."

It was true what the doctor said about focusing on a task, at least when it came to sports.

I spent hours in the backyard, trying to perfect my soccer skills—step-overs, cutbacks, stop-and-gos. I practiced hour after hour, day after day. Sometimes I was focusing on soccer so much I didn't even hear my mom when she called me in for dinner.

I discovered that an Italian cable television station showed games of AC Milan, the European Cup soccer champions. Saturday afternoons became devoted to watching these games, studying the footwork of AC Milan player Roberto Donadoni. I couldn't believe the way the ball seemed almost Velcroed to his foot as he dribbled down the field.

In 1990, when I was eleven years old, America made it to the World Cup for the first time in forty years. I watched the tournament on television. I was thrilled that there were even some New Jersey guys on the team: Tab Ramos and goalkeeper Tony Meola. As my mother rattled pots and boiled water for our evening's mac and cheese, I babbled on and on about the tournament.

Then I headed back outside with my ball to practice some more.

I wanted to make myself faster, stronger, quicker.

From recreational soccer leagues came traveling teams.

I observed that my mom was different from the other parents of kids on those travel teams. Those other parents rolled up to practice in fancy cars. They stood on the sidelines and talked about kitchen renovations and gym memberships. They wore crisp sweaters embroidered with tiny polo players.

I could see my mom didn't feel like she fit in with them. She avoided other parents' eyes when she could. She didn't seem comfortable at all.

I realized something: if she was going to keep bringing me back to this field where she didn't feel comfortable, then I should make her proud. So I'd run even faster, kick even harder.

When I scored a goal, I'd turn to my mom, eager to make sure she'd seen it. She always had.

On Mother's Day, my sixth-grade year, I played striker in a game on a cold, rainy day. Mom stood on the sidelines, apart from the other parents. She held a tiny umbrella for a while, but it was no use. It was raining so hard that the little umbrella did nothing. Mom finally closed it, dropped it to the ground. She held her hands up to shield her eyes from the downpour.

I hadn't gotten her a Mother's Day gift.

She had always done so much for me. She worried about me all the time. She deserved something wonderful. But I didn't have an allowance. I didn't have any money to my name. I couldn't imagine a time when I would ever have enough money to buy flowers or perfume . . . or even a decent umbrella.

But I could play this game for her. I could charge down the field, splashing through puddles as I ran. I could slam that ball past the other team's keeper.

I could score one for our team.

When I did, I turned to her. I threw my arms up in the air, and I shouted over the heads of the other players, "Happy Mother's Day, Mom!"

Even today, all these years and games later, I can still remember the expression that came over her face as she stood there, dripping wet, on the sidelines. That smile on her face, warm against the battleship-gray sky, showed me everything I would ever need to know about love.

CHAPTER 4
MY OWN PRIVATE SOCCER ACADEMY

"ARE YOU READY TO WORK HARDER THAN YOU'VE EVER worked in your life?"

The man in front of me—a short, redheaded Irish guy—had an intense energy. He looked like an over-size kid—the scrappy kind who was always ready for a school-yard fight. The way he was looking at me, I couldn't quite tell if he was planning to train me or eat me.

Mom had brought me here, to the GK1 Club, so I could spend a few hours with Tim Mulqueen. He was the goalkeeping coach of Rutgers University's men's team.

Rutgers was a soccer powerhouse. The previous year, they made it to the NCAA Championship final, losing to UCLA in a penalty kick shoot-out. This year, 1991, they'd been ranked number one.

Tim Mulqueen announced he'd be doing goalkeeping training for youth players, and suddenly parents all over New Jersey were signing their kids up.

Each session cost twenty-five dollars. Mom had scraped together enough cash for a single session with Mulqueen. But that was all she could afford.

Now, here on the field, Mulqueen looked me up and down. "Okay, Tim. Go get in goal."

I started to jog toward the edge of the field.

"Sprint!" Mulqueen called after me. Man, his voice was fierce.

I sprinted.

That afternoon, Mulqueen—Coach Mulch, as he was known to his Rutgers players—pushed me harder than anyone ever had. Other coaches might fire four or five volleys at me at a time. Not Mulch. He hammered ten volleys in a row. Each one came so fast it was hard to get up between them. The moment I saved one, another was already whizzing past me.

"Recover faster," he barked. "You can do better than that."

Then he launched five more rockets.

"Some games are like this," he said. He sent another flying at me.

"They just keep coming at you." And another.

"You've got to be ready." Yet one more.

He watched me carefully during that session. It felt like he was looking at me in a way he hadn't been watching the other kids.

"Move your feet closer together," he said. I did. He kicked a hard low ball at me, and I stopped it.

"Good," he said. "Let's do some more of those."

When my mom came to get me, he ran over to her. "Mrs. Howard," he said, "you've got to bring Tim back."

Mom looked sad. I knew she wanted so many things for me—warmer mittens, math tutors, sessions with a psychologist who could help me with my OCD. She couldn't afford any of those things. So twenty-five dollars a week for goalkeeping training? No way. It was out of the question.

"Your son's got something, Mrs. Howard," said Mulch. "He's got something I haven't seen."

I let those words sink in. I had something.

When Mom didn't answer, Mulch said, "I don't care about the money. Just bring him back. No charge. Ever."

To this day, I believe that offer—to work with me, for free, indefinitely—was as important, as life altering, as any offer I've ever had.

As we walked toward the car, Mulch called after me, "See you next week, Tim Howard!" Then he added, sharply, "Don't be late!"

I trained with Mulch week after week. Eventually, we'd work together every day, year after year. The man was true to his word: he never asked for a single penny.

Within a year, a wealthy New Jersey family put together a club team, hand-selecting the county's—and then later the state's—best young players to surround their own son on the field. Mulch was the guy they hired to coach us.

Mulch was proud of how tough he was on players. In fact, his practices were so brutal that kids often vomited on the field. Over time, it became a kind of joke: practice hadn't started until someone has thrown up.

But of all those kids, Mulch pushed me the hardest.

Everybody on that field had to be excellent; Mulch wanted me to be perfect. More than that, I had to be responsible for other kids' performances, as well as my own.

When other kids played badly, Mulch would jog over to me. "This is on you, Tim. Fix it."

Me? I was standing all the way back here. I couldn't help what was happening in midfield.

"Come on," he'd push. "How do you make it better?"

I watched them for a minute.

"Well," I said, "the defenders are leaving big gaps in the middle. That's how the other team keeps breaking through."

"Right," Mulch said. "So talk to your teammates. Tell them what they need to do differently."

If a kid came to practice even forty seconds late, Mulch yelled at me. "Go have a word with him."

"Why me?"

"'Cause I'm making you the leader. Go."

And if I hesitated even a moment—if I stood there blinking, wondering, *Why is that my job?*—Mulch would holler, "What the heck's the matter with you? Go!"

Once, when our club team—the Central Jersey Cosmos—played a game in southern Jersey, a few of the families got stuck in traffic on the way down. Mulch jogged over to me as I put my cleats on. "Four of your teammates are late, Tim." He was furious.

"Yeah," I said. "I know."

He stood there with his arms folded.

"And?" I said. I was ready to go warm up.

"And so *you* don't get to play," Mulch said.

"What?" He had to be kidding.

His face was dead serious, though.

"Nope. Not when your teammates are late like this."

"But that's not fair!" I hadn't been late. It wasn't like

I had any control over other kids' parents. Besides, there was no one on that team—no one—who was half as good a keeper as I was. He was putting the whole team in jeopardy.

"So I want you to make sure no one is ever late for a game again," he said.

As I moved up the ranks of youth soccer, Mom drove me all over the state, and eventually all over the East Coast, for my different teams.

Although I continued to play midfield on my school teams, I became a full-time goalkeeper everywhere else. I had learned to appreciate the goalkeeping position. It's a *thinking* position. Like with a game of chess, you have to anticipate three moves ahead, then set up the defense to prevent danger.

Then, when danger does come—when the opposing team takes a shot—you have to fly between the ball and the net, doing everything humanly possible to stop it.

The night before we left for a tournament or a game, I'd have to pack and repack my bag. Obsessively. I'd zip it up, then lie in bed. Then I'd get up and do it again.

It's good now, I'd tell myself. *Leave it alone. Just go to sleep.*

But in the same way my OCD drove me to touch household items in a particular pattern, there was a right way to pack my bag, and a wrong way. Somehow I'd know—with that same mounting sense of dread—that I'd packed it the wrong way. So I'd get out of bed, unzip my bag, and start all over.

Not right yet. Do it again.

Then I'd lie in bed and try to shut out the thoughts that kept intruding.

Nope. Still wrong. Try again.

There was always a team hotel somewhere, but it was usually too expensive for Mom. She and I stayed separately in motels a notch down in quality—our motels were always on strips lined with fast-food restaurants and car dealers and pawnshops. Instead of eating out, we'd look for a grocery store. There, we bought store-brand peanut butter and jelly. In the motel room, we'd make a pile of sandwiches and eat them while we watched television.

I didn't mind being somewhere other than the team hotel. There was something special about these stays—just me and Mom.

When I was thirteen, I was selected for the Olympic Development Program. That became my pathway to the Youth National Team.

All of us had been the best in our towns . . . then our counties . . . then our states . . . then our regions. The fact that we were here, at Youth National Team trainings, was confirmation: we were now best in the nation.

It felt pretty good—especially as a kid with TS who sometimes got laughed at by other kids.

I knew that if I could move up the ranks of the Youth National Team, if I could just hang in there and not get cut, I stood a decent chance of making the senior team. That would mean I could play in World Cups.

So I was determined to outrank every other player.

On my way to that goal, I had some things in my favor.

First, I had Mulch driving me.

Then, I had grown up in a rough-and-tumble neighborhood that was filled with every kind of sport, often with kids who were older, bigger, and faster—completely out of my league.

Finally, I had this weird brain that hyperfocused on sports, pushing me to do things again and again. My brain never let me rest—it obsessed. I had to repeat actions until they felt right—even then, "right" was something that I couldn't define if I wanted to. Never mind if the ball went where it was supposed to. All I knew was that I recognized "right" when I felt it. It didn't matter what a save looked like to anyone else. It had to feel perfect. Precise.

That weird brain of mine made all the difference.

CHAPTER 5
"IT WILL TAKE A NATION OF MILLIONS TO HOLD ME BACK"

THE WORLD WAS STUNNED WHEN FIFA ANNOUNCED THAT THE
1994 World Cup would be held in the United States. After
all, America was *not* a soccer country.

Truth is, it was pretty much the only non-soccer
country on the planet.

There was a condition to our hosting the World Cup,
though: we had to launch a major professional soccer
league. Both the World Cup and the league that grew out
of it would have a profound influence on my life.

I'd always followed all the big sports, particularly
the local teams, like the New York Giants and New York
Knicks. But it was hard to follow soccer. After all, soccer

was rarely shown on television. Even then, it was shown mostly in highlights.

So when my friends and I played pickup sports, we never pictured ourselves as soccer players. Instead, we imagined Patrick Ewing or John Starks, or Phil Simms or Lawrence Taylor—players in the NBA or NFL.

But the '94 World Cup, which took place when I was fifteen years old, made the world of international soccer seem closer than ever.

I cheered my heart out for the USA.

Tony Meola, the goalkeeper I'd followed in 1990, was back, as was midfielder Tab Ramos.

I even got to attend a World Cup game in California with the Youth National Team—USA vs. Colombia. It was the only game the US won.

Mulch was a scout for that one, and he sat next to me in the stadium. During that game, he kept pointing to Tony Meola. "That should be you," he said. "Someday, I want it to be you out there."

And just to make sure that I understood, he looked me in the eye. "One of these days, that's going to be you."

In 1995, my Youth National Team qualified for the Under-17 World Championship—our equivalent of the World Cup. It would be held in Ecuador.

The US Soccer Federation told us we'd see poverty

like we hadn't seen before. They also reminded us that we were representing our country and we were to be respectful.

They gave us some spending money. I think it was ten dollars a day, which felt like unbelievable riches to me.

In that tournament, we lost all three games in the group stage—to Japan, Ecuador, and Ghana. But although we were outclassed, I came home with three things I hadn't had before.

First, I had a taste for soccer on the international stage.

Second, I had a new appreciation for all that my mom, Chris, and I had in our little apartment complex. I had thought that my family was poor. Now, for the first time, I understood how lucky we were.

Third, I had around two hundred dollars in my pocket. I hadn't spent any of the money US Soccer had provided. I gave it to my mom so she could use it for groceries and clothes. It was the least I could do, I figured, after all she'd done for us.

Meanwhile, my TS symptoms continued.

Sometimes in class, I heard kids whisper. *Watch Tim. He's going to jerk his head.*

Watch Tim, he's going to twitch.

Just to spite them, I focused all my attention on not having a tic. At the front of the classroom, the teacher was rambling on about the math lesson. I wasn't listening. I was too busy pretending that the urge to tic wasn't welling up inside of me until I was about to burst.

Eventually, when I couldn't hold back any longer, I jumped up and went to the bathroom. There, I let loose, relieved to be left in peace to twitch and cough, to move around and make noise freely.

But when I trained with the Youth National Team, I got to do more than step out of class for a few minutes. I missed school for several weeks at a stretch, several times a year, as I traveled the globe for trainings and games.

These weren't glamorous trips. We stayed in barebones motels. During one trip to Chile, the hotel rooms were so cold that we all had to sleep in parkas . . . and even then we couldn't stay warm!

Also, the coaches and administrators scrutinized everything we did. They watched how we traveled, what we wore. They judged how respectful we were toward them. They watched how we treated one another. I could tell they were sizing up our potential to represent the nation as senior players one day.

I made friends. I especially clicked with the guys from California—I liked their laid-back, casual vibe. Although they were strong on the field, they never seemed to be in a hurry off the field.

I became friends with Nick Rimando, a fellow keeper. He was a jolly prankster in the locker room and reliable and solid on the field. I also liked a kid named Carlos Bocanegra. Carlos looked like he could be a member of a boy band—he had gel in his hair, hoop earrings, and big baggy jeans. In the hotel rooms, Nick, Carlos, and I pulled our fair share of stupid pranks. We filled garbage cans with water, leaned them up against other players' doors, then knocked and ran. By the time those other players opened their doors, water tumbling into their room, we'd be back in our own room, cracking up.

I still felt the shame that made me try to hide my TS. But on the soccer field and basketball court, I was comfortable. That was where I felt at home.

By continuing to play for my high school teams, I gained skills that I still use in every game I play.

I played striker on my high school team. This helped me understand field play. Today, I can anticipate what a striker might do, because I myself *was* one for so many years. My time on the basketball court was useful, too; it made me a more explosive athlete. It helped me react faster.

If I'd grown up in a soccer nation, I would have been

encouraged to focus solely on my soccer skills.

Instead, in America, I became the best all-around athlete that I could.

I knew of only one other person on this earth with Tourette Syndrome: an NBA player named Mahmoud Abdul-Rauf, the point guard for the Denver Nuggets. I'd seen Mahmoud whoop on the basketball court. It was just his tic, but the referees didn't always understand. Sometimes he earned technicals for his outbursts. I'd seen him startle his teammates or opponents with his grunting.

But I'd also seen him dazzle people on the court. He could nail one three-pointer after another.

In interviews, Abdul-Rauf described touching things in certain patterns. He talked about his obsessive drive to make everything feel exactly *right*. Sometimes, that meant tapping or jerking his head. Sometimes it meant putting on his clothes in a precise order. Sometimes it meant practicing his skills over and over again, until he led the league in free-throw percentage.

It confused everyone else. A major sports figure with Tourette Syndrome? But how could anyone be sure he wouldn't have an episode at the wrong moment and cost his team the game?

It didn't confuse me, though. I understood. I

understood the way the symptoms faded in those critical moments. I understood *everything* he described.

To a high school kid with TS, an aspiring athlete myself, Abdul-Rauf was inspiring.

If this guy can be a pro, I thought, *maybe I can, too.*

Coach Mulch continued to push me on the field. He never left me alone.

He was my guide to the tactical. *When the ball comes in from the left, you look to the right; that's where you're going to find your open players.*

He was my guide to the physical. *Feet closer together. Drop down faster. Now get up; that ball is coming right back.*

He was my guide to the mental. *Let that ball come to you, Tim. Don't rush toward it.*

He was my guide to the practical. *Ball goes over the post? Don't go get it right away. You'll feel pressure to go get it, but don't rush. Talk to your defenders. Use the moment as a mini time-out. Go get the ball only after you've told your teammates what you have to say.*

While some keepers are tempted to punt the ball down the field, particularly in the final minutes of the game—just do anything to send it as far away as possible—Mulch taught me to stop and think. *Throw the ball if you can. When you throw it, you have control over where it goes. And when you throw it, send it right to your teammate's feet.*

If I didn't get it exactly right—if, say, I threw it to a player and he gained control with his chest, or his thigh—Mulch insisted that I do it all over again.

"That was a terrible throw, Tim. Get it to his feet."

The guy was relentless in his demand for perfection. Which, actually, was a pretty good fit for an OCD kid like myself.

Major League Soccer (MLS) began its play in 1996, the year I turned seventeen.

All the big names from the US National Team from the 1994 World Cup signed on, and a few international stars from the World Cup, too. Tab Ramos and Tony Meola, the New Jersey guys who'd been in the World Cup, joined the New York/New Jersey MetroStars.

The league had some bizarre rules meant to appeal to American audiences. Official time was kept on a clock that counted backward, not forward. No game ended in a tie; there was a shoot-out at the end of any tied game to determine the winner. Salaries for most players were hardly what you would think of as major league.

But I didn't care. The MLS was a tangible goal.

Then Mulch was hired as the goalkeeping coach for the MetroStars—as well as for the New Jersey Imperials.

The Imperials was like a minor league team associated with the MLS club.

My Mulch! Coaching professional soccer!

I felt my little world getting closer to the one I'd only dared imagine.

We were getting to the end of high school, and I had some decisions to make. Because of my athletic skills, I'd had some interest from colleges. But, nationwide, some players were heading straight from high school to the MLS.

Mulch sat down with me and my mom. He explained that I could start playing on the New Jersey Imperials, and if all went well, I might be able to move up to the MetroStars—the MLS—the following season.

He asked my mom what she thought, and she said it was up to me.

I wanted to go pro as soon as possible. Soccer careers are so short, I didn't dare wait.

It was a big risk. Even if I could make it to the MLS, there was no established career path for an American soccer player. It wasn't like the NBA or the NFL.

This was a total leap of faith.

I played so many games during those years, I couldn't count them if I tried.

But there's only one that goes down in local folklore, and it wasn't even a soccer game.

North Brunswick's biggest basketball rival is St. Joseph's High School. My senior year, St. Joe's had this big-time player, a sophomore that everyone kept talking about: Jay Williams. Later, Jay would play for Duke and be the number-two pick in the NBA draft by the Chicago Bulls. My North Brunswick basketball team had a good run that year—good enough that we were heading to the county championships. Our opponent? St. Joe's.

I would be guarding Jay.

If you ask my old coaches what happened that night, they'll tell you all about how I shut down the great Jay Williams. They'll swear by it, saying things like *Tim owned Jay . . . that game is proof that Tim could have played in the NBA.*

But I was there. I know what the reality was.

I had some strong plays, including one critical block during the game's final minutes. And it's true we won the championship that year.

I'm telling you, though: Jay was breathtaking, just a perfect blend of agility, grace, ball handling, and explosive ability. I was used to being the strongest athlete around. But Jay was the best I'd ever seen on the court—you can't guard a guy like Jay; all you can do is try to keep up.

That feeling I had playing against him was one I wouldn't have again for six years.

The next time, I'd be standing on a soccer field in Lisbon, Portugal, watching a teenager named Cristiano Ronaldo . . . who later became the best in the world.

In 1997, I signed with the New Jersey Imperials, and started playing games three months before I graduated from high school.

"You remember everything I taught you about taking leadership?" Mulch asked.

"Yeah."

"It won't be fun and games anymore. Once you're a pro, you'll be responsible for other people's livelihoods," he said.

He narrowed his eyes. "You'd darn well better not forget what I've taught you."

I wouldn't. In my high school yearbook, my graduation photo sits above a single quote, inspired by the title of a rap album I liked back then. "It will take a nation of millions to hold me back."

CHAPTER 6
STILL LEARNING

ALTHOUGH I ONLY MADE A TINY BIT OF MONEY PLAYING FOR the Imperials, I was so happy. I was a professional athlete. I was earning a paycheck . . . for playing soccer!

I got a beat-up old car. It was tiny and noisy, and it had spots of rust above the exhaust. But to this day, that first car is still my favorite of all time.

The Imperials had some local legends, guys who had been college stars. But we also had players who worked long hours as plumbers and pipe fitters in the Bronx and Long Island City, then commuted out to New Jersey to train with us. Some were nearly twice my age.

We practiced on a field next to the Hackensack River.

Each day when we arrived, the field was covered with Canadian geese. We had to start doing ball drills to shoo the birds away. However, they always left reminders of their presence on the grass. I probably ran through hundreds of pounds of goose poop in those days!

Our locker room was similar to the one at my high school, and our "uniforms" were basic, 1950s-style gray cotton T-shirts. The team had no money for flights, so we rode a bus up and down the East Coast, from Vermont to Myrtle Beach, South Carolina. After each game, we'd load the front seat with pizza boxes. The Irish players sang songs at the back of the bus, and the rest of us joined in.

Not many people came to our games, so the league occasionally pulled a stunt to draw larger crowds. At my first away game, against the Myrtle Beach SeaDawgs, they invited a guest player: Laura Davies, the English professional golfer, who was in town for a golf tournament. To be eligible to play in the game, she'd signed a four-year contract with the SeaDawgs, worth a whopping one dollar.

The stunt worked; the game attracted over 2,220 fans—far more than our usual audience of family members and friends. And I've got to hand it to Laura Davies: she had some nice touches on that ball.

We were a ragtag team in an unglamorous league. But Mulch was the coach, and he ran us like we were AC Milan.

That year was fantastic for me. I played a lot of games and got a ton of experience in goal.

Not all of those experiences were ones to be proud of, though.

One time, one of my teammates scored a great goal. I ran to midfield to congratulate him, and while I stood there, the other team kicked off and launched the ball into my empty net.

Thank goodness *that* game wasn't on television . . . and that it happened in the days before YouTube.

Playing for the Imperials allowed me to make mistakes—and to learn from them—knowing there would never be more than a couple of hundred people to witness them.

Mulch's plan for me worked, because after that season on the Imperials, I headed to the big leagues; I joined the MetroStars for their 1998 season.

When the MLS was formed, everyone expected the MetroStars to dominate. After all, they had so many great players: Tab Ramos. Roberto Donadoni. Tony Meola. They had a guy named Alexi Lalas. Famous for his wild mop of fiery red hair, Lalas had been the first American ever to play in the Italian Serie A.

They were some very big personalities.

First of all, there was Tab, who was as serious as it

got. Guys might be horsing around, loosening up with a game of "soccer tennis"—they'd tape a line down the center of the locker room, knocking the soccer ball back and forth like a tennis match. But when Tab walked in, or decided things were too out of control, he'd cut that game short with one word: "Enough."

All of us obeyed.

Then there was Alexi Lalas. Alexi was like the opposite of Tab; he was outgoing and always ready for a laugh. Alexi loved blasting loud music when he was in the shower. As he was singing along from behind the shower curtain, Tab would walk over and snap off the radio without speaking.

Then Alexi would step out of the shower dripping wet. He'd turn it back on even louder. Tab's face would burn red.

And then there was Tony Meola. Man, I was terrified of Tony. He was a hulking presence, with enormous biceps and a chest as broad as a truck.

After the 1994 World Cup, Tony tried out for the New York Jets, nearly nabbing a spot as a placekicker. And his personality was equally big and brash. He wasn't afraid to let everyone know that he was the best. And man, when Tony was mad—which was often—he could make guys cower.

Keepers train together. One stands in goal while the others fire shots at him. But when Tony sent balls toward me, they either flew past my head or skidded past me on the ground. I dove all over the box trying to stop them.

I failed, and Tony rolled his eyes.

And when I kicked balls at him, Tony quickly grew exasperated. My accuracy was off. My shots didn't have enough power.

"What the heck is that?" he snapped on more than one occasion. "That was a terrible ball."

Or worse, he'd remind me that I shouldn't be there at all.

"This isn't high school, you know," he'd sneer.

Once, he turned to Mulch in frustration, throwing a hand in my direction. "My performance is dropping off training with this guy. He needs to do better."

Later, Mulch said quietly to me, "Just do what you do, Timmy. You keep your head. Be a good teammate. Be yourself. He'll come around."

Maybe, I thought. *But I'm not so sure.*

I tried to be friendly.

"Good luck, Tony," I always said before games.

Or, "Have a good game, Tony!"

If he responded at all, it was always just a quick

"Thanks." He'd mutter it in a low voice, and he wouldn't even look at me. More often than not, though, Tony didn't respond at all.

Not a word, not a glance, not a nod. He just pulled on his gloves and walked away as if I hadn't said a thing.

A good attacking player will gladly hit a hundred shots in a row at you if you let them. Tab did that for me. He and I stayed on the field as everyone else headed to the locker rooms. Each of us practiced our game skills.

At first, many of his balls whizzed past my head. After a while, I got better at stopping his shots.

Then we did it some more, and I began to save the majority of them. I tracked my progress. I dove, I reached, I stretched. Whether I saved it or watched it fly past, I got up and walked back to my line, ready to do the whole thing again.

Keepers can shine when their team is losing . . . and the MetroStars gave Tony plenty of chances to shine. We were a terrible team . . . so bad that some people thought the team was cursed!

Thank goodness we had Tony as our goalkeeper. He was terrific.

In August, though, Tony argued with a referee. He was fined $1,500 for "major game misconduct" and was slapped with a one-game suspension. Until then, Tony had played every minute of the season's previous twenty-four games. Now he'd be missing the home game in Giants Stadium against the Colorado Rapids. The Metro-Stars would have to rely on the number-two goalkeeper to save the day.

Me.

When I get nervous or excited, my tics go crazy. In the moments leading up to my first MLS game, I probably cleared my throat about five hundred times.

In the locker room, on my stool, I found a handwritten note.

Tony's handwriting.

YOU'RE GOING TO DO GREAT TODAY. TONY

Even Tab seemed to be warming up to me. Just before the game started, he looked me in the eye. "This is not the most important game you're going to play," he said.

Not exactly effusive, mind you. But for Tab, that was as warm and fuzzy as it got.

I cleared my throat again. "Thanks."

There's pretty much just one moment I remember from that game. It was the sixty-third minute, and the MetroStars were ahead when striker Wolde Harris came racing toward me. Wolde was one of the top MLS scorers back then. He was just yards from the goal when he fired a hard shot a few feet to my right.

It's almost impossible for a striker to miss from that close. I think everyone thought for sure that it was going in.

But Tony had been launching rockets at me for five months. My reflexes were sharp. I reached out my right hand and stopped that thing, cold.

All these years later, that remains one of my favorite saves of all time. I still remember how it felt when my hand first made contact with the ball. I knew that I'd just blocked a point-blank shot in my MLS debut.

And I was thrilled.

A half hour later, we walked off the field. We'd won! Tony stood in the tunnel, dressed in street clothes. He literally ran toward me and wrapped his arms around me in a tight hug. It was like getting hugged by a grizzly bear.

"That was great, Tim," he said. His voice was so happy—so unlike the Tony I'd been seeing all these months. "That was really, really great!"

And that game changed everything for me and Tony. After that, he became like my big brother, always looking out for me.

Unfortunately, he wouldn't be with the team much longer.

* * *

The MetroStars slumped badly as the season progressed. We led the league in ejections, with nine, and we ranked third in yellow cards. We got a new coach, Bora Milutinović, who had already led four countries into the second round of the World Cup—Mexico in '86, Costa Rica in '90, the US in '94, and Nigeria in '98.

Bora had his work cut out for him. He shook up the team. He traded Tony and Alexi to Kansas City. Tony was replaced with Mike Ammann, a jokester who always made us laugh.

But Bora's efforts were no more successful than any other coach's had been. We continued to lose. By June of 1999, our record was 4–9, the worst in the Eastern Conference.

On June 20 of that year we played the Kansas City Wizards. Their record was 3–10. They were the bottom team in the Western Conference.

So this was the opposite of a championship match. We were two losing teams, battling it out to see which of us was the worst of the worst.

They embarrassed us 6–0.

We were the worst of the worst, it turned out.

CHAPTER 7
GROWING UP

MIKE AMMANN CAME AND WENT. BY 2001, NOT LONG AFTER I turned twenty-two, I became the starting keeper for the MetroStars.

By this point, I had not told my teammates—or anyone else—about my Tourette Syndrome. I still tried to hide it.

But I was tired of hiding it.

I'd been thinking a lot recently about Mahmoud Abdul-Rauf. He had meant so much to me back when I was a teenager. It genuinely helped knowing there was someone else out there with TS—a pro athlete at that. But Abdul-Rauf had left the NBA in 1998, and I knew of no other pros—no other public figures at all—with TS.

What about the kids with TS who were out there right now? What if one of them might need to know that other people have TS, too?

I approached the MetroStars' publicity director and said I wanted to come out publicly with having Tourette Syndrome. He looked surprised. It was as if he didn't understand what I was saying. Then I saw the lightbulb go off for him: Oh, *that's* what's going on. *That's* why he's always clearing his throat. *That's* why he's so twitchy.

I told him something else, too: I told him I wanted to work with kids in the community who had TS. I asked him if he could help me find an organization that I could work with.

He put me in touch with Faith Rice, who was launching a new organization to help New Jersey families affected by TS.

When I called Faith, she told me that her own son, Kim, had TS, and that she'd spent two decades running herself ragged trying to help him.

She wanted her organization to do two things. First, she wanted to raise awareness about TS, so people could recognize and understand it. Second, she wanted to give kids with TS the support they needed—all the support her own son hadn't had.

* * *

When the MetroStars announced that their starting keeper had Tourette Syndrome, it became big news. Stories about me appeared in major newspapers—the *Daily News*, New Jersey's *Star-Ledger*, *USA Today*. I got an eight-hundred-word feature in the *New York Times* Sports Sunday. A profile in *Sports Illustrated*. I was also on television.

Faith put me right to work, too.

I began to host events for kids with TS. Families came to a MetroStars game, and then we'd all eat lunch together. At these events, I told families about my own Tourette Syndrome—about sitting in the classroom trying not to tic. Then I answered kids' questions.

I still remember the first time I looked out into one of those crowds of kids. It was an important moment for me.

As I talked, I saw a lot of movement—head jerks and quick arm motions, leg kicks and eye blinks, and sometimes even a kid hitting himself in the head. I heard some noises I didn't usually hear—coughs, hums, hoots, my own words being echoed in another's voice.

But looking out over the audience, I understood that these were just kids. They happened to have TS, but they were the same as any other kids out there.

If they were remarkable at all, it was for how wonderfully ordinary they were.

And if their TS didn't make them different—if they were just regular kids—that meant that I had been a regular kid, too. All those times I'd tried to hide my TS, all those times I'd been ashamed, I hadn't needed to be.

"I'm Tim Howard," I said to that room. "I have Tourette Syndrome. I live with TS. I try to excel with TS. What I don't do is suffer from TS. And you don't have to either."

After the event, a girl approached me. She was probably fifteen years old, with dark eyes. At one point during my talk, I'd seen her jerk her head so hard that her glasses fell to the floor.

"Hey," she quipped. "Nice haircut."

It was a joke. By that point, I'd started shaving my head completely. I laughed out loud, taken aback by her confidence.

"I'm Marisa," she said. "I think it's pretty cool what you're doing."

We talked for a while. Marisa went to a high school not far from my own high school. She wanted to travel the world. She was a golfer. She earned straight As. She was smart and confident.

And yet I was sure there were people in her life who would never see past the surface of her symptoms. There would probably always be people in her life who judged her.

Such a funny disorder, I thought. That the surface of

a person—their tics—should hide their core, the parts of them that really matter.

Actually, I realized, that's probably true for many things: people see the surface only, instead of what lies beneath.

I played every minute of every game that season.

I still got scored on plenty. I remember, for example, a San Jose rookie named Landon Donovan netting his first-ever MLS goal against me that season.

But I finished strong. I had 1.33 goals against average, meaning in each game I let in an average of just 1.33 goals. That's an impressive record, especially considering how much time the MetroStars spent defending our goal. By the end of the season, I was named to the MLS All-Stars, and I was voted MLS Goalkeeper of the Year, the youngest-ever MLS player to earn that honor. I was also selected as part of the league's "Best XI."

Perhaps most rewarding of all, I was named MLS Humanitarian of the Year for my work with kids with TS.

Even today, the honors I've won on behalf of the TS community remain my favorite ones.

By my fourth season with the MetroStars, I wanted something bigger. I wanted fiercer competition.

I wanted to go to Europe.

There are spectacular soccer players all over the world. Nearly all of them aspire to play in the top leagues of Europe—the English Premier League, the German Bundesliga, the Spanish La Liga, the Italian Serie A, and the Portuguese Primeira Liga among them.

Those are the leagues where the competition is the toughest.

In Europe, a player can aspire to be the greatest in the world.

It's tough to make it there. European teams, called clubs, have youth academies, which are like intense talent factories. There, kids as young as seven are trained by top-tier pro coaches and trainers. Clubs spend millions of dollars on these academies, and each year, some kids are cut, and new prodigies are brought in. They are intense, serious places. There's not a lot of joy there, not a lot of fun. But if kids can make it all the way through, they become world-class players.

Clubs also scour the globe for potential players— scouts trek through jungles in Brazil and remote outposts in Africa, looking for players who can be groomed into great professional players. Meanwhile, ambitious and talented players send videotapes and résumés to clubs.

It's supercompetitive. It's a very tough talent pool to get noticed in.

But in four years, I'd gone from being a high school

kid to one of the top players in the MLS. During my call-ups to training camps with the US National Team, I played side by side with Kasey Keller and Brad Friedel, two goalkeepers who were already playing in Europe.

They'd managed to do it. I could too.

I got an agent, Dan, who immediately got to work trying to find me a club where I could play.

Dan got me an invitation to train for two weeks at a Dutch club called Feyenoord—a very good club—at the end of the MLS season. If they liked me, he said, they might want me to sign on as a player.

I felt confident; I was physically and mentally ready. I took an overnight flight to Holland. Instead of resting when I arrived, I headed straight into my first training session. That's how pumped I was.

It was a good two weeks. I trained my butt off. I liked the team, and I genuinely felt like I fit in. By the end, I really expected that Feyenoord would want to make an offer.

But they didn't. Instead, they said that they liked me and that they thought I had great potential . . . but they just didn't feel sure enough.

They said they would continue tracking me.

I was so disappointed, but what could I do? I decided that I would push to be the best goalkeeper in MLS for a few more years. I'd try to push my way into the US

National Team. Eventually, I hoped, I'd be good enough to get an offer from Feyenoord . . . or some other European club.

But it wouldn't be long before I'd get a phone call that would change everything.

CHAPTER 8
"WE'VE GOT OUR EYES ON YOU"

THE YEAR 2002 WAS A BIG ONE FOR ME.

It was another World Cup year. I was the number-four keeper in that World Cup, behind Kasey Keller, Brad Friedel, and Tony Meola. I didn't get to attend the tournament, but I watched it closely.

Some of my own teammates played, though. For example, Clint Mathis. Clint had joined the MetroStars a few seasons ago. He'd transferred from the LA Galaxy. Everyone loved Clint. When he scored his first goal for the MetroStars, he'd lifted up his jersey to reveal an "I ♥ NY" T-shirt. The fans ate it up.

Before Clint left for the tournament, he shaved his

head into a Mohawk. In that World Cup, he scored a sensational goal against South Korea in their home stadium, earning the US a 1–1 draw. In that instant, Mathis looked like the best striker on earth. Clint helped the US team to advance to the knockout stage. There, we beat our archrival Mexico.

By the time the US team came home, Clint had become the face of American soccer. He appeared on the covers of *Sports Illustrated* and *ESPN* magazine, and even bantered on television about how to grow out a Mohawk.

It was so exciting to see my teammate become famous like that.

That year, I also had my first cap with the US National Team—the first time I represented the US on the senior men's team. We played in Birmingham, and my first game was a shutout. I made three saves, and we won, 1–0.

Around that time, I fell in love. Laura was from Memphis, the cousin of one of my teammates. We stayed up all night talking, and that was it. From that moment on, we started talking every day, for hours.

Right from the start, I knew we'd be together for a long, long time. Within a few months, we started imagining getting a dog together.

"Let's name him Clayton," she said, and I agreed.

And then we were imagining children, too.

"I've always wanted a son named Jacob," she said. Once again, I agreed.

I felt carefree and warm and open around her.

Laura was easy to talk to, easy to laugh with. And so, so easy to fall in love with.

Meanwhile, the end of that MetroStars season was anything but easy.

We still weren't clicking as a team. We still weren't winning.

I was starting to worry that we never would.

We lost our three final games of the year. We also led the league in red cards, with a total of nine. In the second-to-last game of the season, against DC United, both Clint Mathis and I earned red cards. We had to sit out the last match, cringing together as we watched the team lose 3–0 to the New England Revolution.

That final defeat made us one of only two MLS teams that failed to reach the play-offs.

That's when the MetroStars announced that we'd be getting a new coach: a guy named Bob Bradley.

As the 2003 season kicked off, things were going well.

I adored Laura, I really liked our new coach, Bob Bradley, and I was getting noticed by the national team.

Then one day, still early in the season, my phone

rang. It was a number I didn't recognize—an overseas number. When I answered, the voice on the other side spoke quickly, in a crisp British accent.

"Tim Howard? Tony Coton here. I'm the goalkeeping coach at Manchester United. We've seen some tapes of you play, and we're a bit interested. No need to do anything. Just wanted to let you know we've got our eyes on you. Maybe we'll even come see you play sometime down the road. Take care."

When you get a call like that, there's a delay between when you hear the words and when you understand them.

British voice . . . not a name I know . . . Manchester United.

And then: Holy cow. Manchester United.

After that, I barely registered what was said.

Interested, he said. He said they were interested.

It was Tony who did all the talking. I probably managed an "okay" or "thanks." Then I mumbled good-bye. After we hung up, I stood there staring at the phone for a long moment.

It had happened so fast. Part of me wondered if the call had happened at all.

Manchester United was the most famous club in the world. Man U held the record for the most English Premier League titles: fifteen in total! Seven of those were in the previous decade alone.

Just a few years ago, Man U had become the first team in history to win a "continental treble"—the Premier League title, the FA Cup, and the UEFA Champions League title, all in a single season.

Man U not only attracted stars, they made stars.

Irish legend George Best, the so-called "fifth Beatle" who inspired the line, "Maradona good, Pele Great, George Best?" had played for Man U. Peter Schmeichel, one of the greatest goalkeepers of all time, was also a Man U guy. Bobby Charlton, Eric "the King" Cantona, David Beckham—all played for United.

The manager (and coach), Sir Alex Ferguson, had even been knighted for his services to English soccer.

Manchester United could have any goalkeeper in the world.

And I was just a twenty-three-year-old kid from New Jersey.

I had some talent. I had potential. But I was young.

I mean, Feyenoord hadn't felt compelled to sign me.

I had yet to play in any international match of consequence.

I called Laura. I could scarcely believe the words coming out of my mouth: Manchester United. Tony Coton. Said they're watching me.

"Oh, my goodness, Tim!" she exclaimed. There was so much warmth and excitement in her voice. "That's so great!"

Later, she confessed that she'd immediately called her brother after we spoke. "Hey, Jerry?" she asked. "What's Manchester United?"

During the MetroStars preseason in March of 2003, I was selected as an alternate keeper for the US National Team game against Venezuela.

Kasey Keller would be there, too. We'd train together for a week.

I explained to Laura just how big this was.

Kasey had been playing in England's Premier League for over a decade now; he was a veteran of three World Cups.

"He's an outstanding keeper, one of the best," I told her. "During a 1998 game against Brazil, he made ten saves. Some from point-blank range. Can you even imagine? Ten saves!"

It was true. Brazil was one of the best teams on the planet. But we'd won that game. And Kasey had earned the US a shutout—no goals conceded.

Kasey turned out to be a great guy. He was competitive, but also friendly. He was a world-class player, yet he didn't bring a shred of ego to the field.

During training, if I made a hard save, he always complimented me.

"Really great," he might say. I could tell he meant it.

I watched Kasey get ready for the Venezuela match. The guy was totally relaxed. No clenched jaw, no apparent jitters—exactly as if he'd been hanging out in the locker room.

I wished him luck. "Thanks, Tim," he said, very friendly.

I realized something then: everything that could happen in this sport had already happened to him.

Over the course of his career, Kasey had faced thousands of shots. They'd flown at him from every angle, every swerve, every speed.

He'd stared down the best strikers on earth. There was nothing left that could surprise Kasey. He'd seen it all before.

Watching Kasey reminded me of how I'd felt as a kid playing against my brother's friends. I remembered wanting to be as good as they were.

Now I wanted to be as good as Kasey.

No. I wanted to be better.

Meanwhile, I kept thinking about that call from Tony Coton. *Maybe we'll come see you play sometime. We've got our eyes on you.*

* * *

In March, I was scheduled to play in a US-Mexico friendly game in Houston. It would also be the first match between the two teams since we'd knocked Mexico out of the World Cup the previous year.

I learned that Tony Coton was planning to come to the game.

He wanted to see me play in that match.

The US-Mexico rivalry is one of the fiercest rivalries in all of soccer.

For a long time, Mexico was clearly the better team. Mexico dominated CONCACAF—the Confederation of North, Central American, and Caribbean Association Football. When we played them, it was assumed that Mexico would win.

But in recent decades, the US had steadily improved.

Since 1999, we'd had six clean sheets—games in which the opposing team doesn't score on us—against Mexico on home soil. In 483 minutes of play, we hadn't conceded a single goal to our fiercest rivals.

Then we'd beaten them in the World Cup.

The game that Tony Coton would see was being called La Revancha en la Cancha. Revenge on the Field.

Mexico was planning to take back their honor.

Most of the seats in the stadium had been snapped up within the first five days of sale—almost entirely by fans of the Mexico team.

A crowd of over sixty thousand was predicted—the largest audience ever for a US home game.

Between the high stakes and Tony Coton's presence in the stands, there would be a whole lot riding on those ninety minutes.

CHAPTER 9
BIG CHANGES

MAY 8. HOUSTON. IT WAS LA REVANCHA EN LA CANCHA—THE game where Tony Coton would watch me play.

Showtime.

As I took my place in goal, I looked out at my teammates. They were some of the greatest guys I knew: Carlos Bocanegra was defending. Clint Mathis was there. So was Landon Donovan, the boy wonder who'd scored his first MLS goal against me in 2001. It was an honor to be there among them.

We can do this, I thought.

Then I looked up at the stands.

The stadium was packed. There were seventy

thousand fans out there. My body nearly vibrated with the noise. The thing is, even though we were playing in America, nearly all those fans were rooting for Mexico. The place was a sea of green Mexico jerseys.

Somewhere in that stadium is Tony Coton, I thought. *He is deciding whether the incredible Manchester United wants me on their team.*

It was a tough game from the start. Mexico packed on the pressure. The Mexico fans made so much noise my defenders literally couldn't hear me shouting at them.

I'd never played a match this intense before.

Twenty-four minutes in, Mexico almost scored. Jesus Arellano sent a hard shot from the edge of the box. The ball veered toward the top corner.

I have a decent vertical leap—something that was always helpful in basketball, too—and I needed every inch of it. I launched myself as high as I could. I got my fingertips to the ball.

I sent it to safety. Barely.

I sure hoped that Tony Coton hadn't taken that exact moment to go to the bathroom, because I was mighty proud of that save.

The game ended in a scoreless draw—a shutout for me.

This is good, I thought. I was so excited to talk with Tony Coton after the game . . . but apparently he'd departed at the final whistle. He'd told Dan, my agent, that he'd seen what he needed to see . . . whatever that meant.

I was going to have to wait.

That same spring, I proposed to Laura. We were going to be married in November, after the MetroStars season ended.

As I waited to hear from Tony Coton, Laura kept me updated on the wedding plans. She made guest lists and arranged seating charts. Already, the invite list was 250 people, and it was swelling every day. One afternoon, Laura called me on the phone, totally giddy.

She'd bought a wedding dress. "I can't wait to marry you in it!" she said.

I couldn't wait to marry her, either.

Then I got the call.

I'd done it. Manchester United wanted me. They made me an offer, a good one.

I'd join their team before the start of the Premier League season. If we could get the paperwork completed on time, I'd be able to play in some preseason matches in the US—first against Juventus in New Jersey, then against Barcelona in Philadelphia. Then we would fly to Portugal to play Sporting Lisbon.

After that, we'd head to England to start the Premier League season.

The Juventus game was in July . . . it was right around the corner!

It was amazing news in all ways but one: the wedding.

In the Premier League, every game matters.

There are twenty teams, and each plays all the others twice—once at home, and once away. That means thirty-eight games over the course of the season, roughly one per week, with only occasional weeks off. Even in those "off" weeks, there are games—for other leagues and tournaments.

There are no play-offs in the Premier League, either. Teams are awarded points for each game—three for a win, one for a draw, and zero for a loss. At the end of the season, the team with the highest number of points is crowned champion.

The winning difference can come down to a single game.

On the losing side, the stakes are even higher. The three teams with the lowest record don't even get to stay in the Premier League. They get relegated to a lower league, and other teams take their place. It would be like if the Chicago Cubs, after one bad season, suddenly disappeared from Major League Baseball—like they might be sent to the minor leagues if their record wasn't good enough.

So players don't miss a game. Ever. Not even to get married to the warmest, most adorable southern girl in America.

Laura and I didn't have a choice. Our wedding plans went on hold.

"But will you actually play?"

So many people asked me the same question. Friends asked. Teammates. MLS staff. Family members.

The question was a polite way of suggesting that I wouldn't.

It made sense, too. After all, I was young and unproven

Also, Manchester United had Fabien Barthez, goalkeeper for the 1998 World Cup champions, France. I assumed I'd sit on the bench and watch Fabien play, just as I had under Tony Meola.

But I was hungry. And I could learn from Fabien, just like I'd learned from Tony.

And this was Manchester United, the greatest soccer club on earth.

The truth is, I'd have gone there to wash cars if they'd asked me.

* * *

Almost immediately, the headlines began appearing:

"United Want American with Brain Disorder"—the *Guardian*

"Manchester United Trying to Sign 'Disabled' Goal-keeper"—the *Independent*

"We Swear It's True: Tourette's Sufferer Is Target for United"—the *Mirror*

I never read the articles below the headlines. I didn't need that kind of garbage cluttering up my brain.

I played my final game for the MetroStars—against the New England Revolution—on Saturday, July 12, 2003.

In the locker room, Coach Bob Bradley announced to the team that I'd be captain for the day. This was a great honor, and a lovely gesture.

Bob had been so decent about the transfer. He'd be losing his starting keeper, but he understood what an opportunity this was for me. "If it were my son," he said— he had a fifteen-year-old son, Michael, who was coming up through the youth team ranks—"I'd want him to play for Manchester United."

I've never forgotten his kindness.

The match turned out to be one of the more memorable of my MetroStars career. We were down 3–0 until the sixty-sixth minute. It looked like a loss for sure. But in the final minutes of the game, we made a fantastic comeback. We ended up tying the Revolution at 3–3.

After the game, I thanked Bob Bradley for every-thing. "I hope we can work together again someday," I said.

He nodded. "Good luck to you, Timmy."

Then Laura and I took an overnight flight to Eng-land.

It was a whirlwind trip, just thirty-six hours long.

After landing, we drove to the Manchester United training ground. The team was on the field, running drills. Right in the middle of them stood Sir Alex Ferguson. He was barking at them—yelling louder, more ferociously, than Bob Bradley ever had.

When he saw us, he stopped training. He introduced me to the team.

"This is Tim Howard," he said to them. "New keeper."

And just like that, I was shaking hands with some of the biggest names in English soccer.

The Neville brothers, Phil and Gary. Paul Scholes, Ryan Giggs, Nicky Butt. Rio Ferdinand. Roy Keane. Ruud van Nistelrooy. Fabien Barthez.

These guys were world-famous. They were super-stars, every one of them. Now they were all right in front of me. In a few hours, after I signed my contract, they'd be my teammates.

The whole thing was downright surreal. It felt like I was stepping straight into a dream.

Next, I had to get medical exams. When a team like Manchester United makes an investment in a player, they want to rule out any surprise medical problems. I shuttled between technicians and physicians. They measured my lung capacity and joint functioning. They took my blood pressure, and then they took my actual blood.

They calculated muscle mass, checked for dental issues. They gave me CT scans, stress tests, an electrocardiogram, and an echocardiogram.

They poked me and prodded me until I felt like a hunk of meat.

But we ruled out any surprises. The deal would go forward.

After that, Laura and I had to find a place to live. Manchester United owned several homes, and we could live in one for a few years.

I'd never lived in a house before—only apartments.

And wow! These Man U homes weren't just any homes, either: they were mansions. We picked a beauty of a home in a neighborhood called Wilmslow. It had six bedrooms, huge bay windows, and skylights. It was far fancier than even the Fox Hill Run homes that I used to marvel at back in Jersey.

Laura and I wrapped our arms around each other in

the driveway. We took pictures.

"I can't believe we just get to move in," she whispered.

"Yeah," I said. "This is crazy."

I tried to picture living there with Laura, but it still felt like imagining someone else's life.

Then we went to Old Trafford—where Manchester United plays, and where their offices are headquartered. There, I signed the contract that changed my life.

And just like that, I jumped from the losing-est team in MLS to one of the best teams in the world's top league. I didn't feel exactly like Cinderella, but the whole thing sure seemed a lot like a fairy tale. I kept wondering when the clock would strike midnight.

On the flight home, Laura and I talked about the wedding. Now that we couldn't have our November wedding, when could we get married?

"You know what we could do . . . ," I said, my voice trailing off.

"What?" she asked.

"We could just get married before I go."

"Before you go?" she asked.

"Yeah," I answered. "Why not?"

"Tim, your first Manchester United game is in a couple of days."

"So let's go to city hall as soon as we land," I said.

Mom picked us up at the airport. Laura and I were giddy as we walked through baggage claim and out to the curb.

"Mom," I said, "can you take us to city hall? We need to get a marriage license."

It rained almost all day, July 18, 2003—except for a few moments around three p.m. But those were the moments that mattered.

That's when Laura and I were married in Central Park, New York City, in a tiny ceremony.

Laura never got to wear the wedding dress she had purchased. It was in a shop in Memphis being altered, so she bought a simple white dress at the mall.

Instead of the planned 250 guests, only ten people were able to get to New York on short notice: both sets of parents; my nana, brother, and young cousin; the Metro-Stars chaplain; a high school buddy; and one friend of Laura's.

Afterward, we celebrated at the Chart House restaurant in Weehawken, directly across the river from Manhattan. We were taking photographs outside when word got around the restaurant that a professional athlete was on the deck. The next thing I knew, strangers started coming out to snap their own shots. Someone on a New York City fireboat noticed all the flashbulbs popping. Without knowing what the occasion was, they pulled up in front of the restaurant.

Before I knew it, the crew was putting on a liquid light show, with enormous colored plumes of water arcing in every direction.

Everything in my life is about to change, I kept thinking. *The world I know, the people I love, I'm leaving it all behind.*

And then I got ready for my first game with Manchester United.

My first match for United would be held, ironically enough, in New Jersey—at Giants Stadium, of all places, where the MetroStars play their home games. When I walked out onto the field, I was shocked. It sure looked like Giants Stadium, the same place I'd played so many times. But it was transformed. This time, the stadium was filled with people—seventy thousand of them.

The atmosphere was electric.

Because it was just a friendly match, Ferguson wanted me to play, instead of their usual keeper, Fabien Barthez.

I remember telling myself that I was taking the whole thing in stride. Maybe anyone who knew me then would agree: they'd say I played it cool. That I didn't get rattled.

That's not true, though. I was anything but cool. I was a nervous wreck.

Just before the game, someone snapped a picture. In the photo, I'm smiling . . . but it's not a confident grin. My smile is shy, even sheepish. I look like a little kid. A little kid asking himself, *Do I even belong here?*

I was surrounded by some of the greatest soccer players in the world. They were waiting to see what I could do.

The whistle was about to blow.

I was completely and totally afraid.

PART TWO

CHAPTER 10
"YOU'RE NOT IN AMERICA ANYMORE, SON"

IT WAS LIKE I'D GONE TO JUPITER.

It felt like I'd rocketed not only into a different league, different country, different culture . . . but onto a different planet altogether.

In this world, flashbulbs popped. Fans swarmed team buses as we arrived at stadiums. They screamed like we were rock stars.

A full-time staff of six hundred supported the work of Manchester United. On game day, those ranks swelled to 1,200—nearly a hundred employees for every player on the field. During our preseason tour of the US, we traveled by private jet, chartered by the club from its owner, the Dallas Mavericks. It was a luxury 767, and it had been fitted with custom leather seats designed for the comfort of even the tallest NBA star.

I remembered those state-to-state bus trips I'd taken with the Imperials. Already, those rides seemed like a million years ago.

We had won all of our friendlies in the US games, but that winning streak ended abruptly when we played Sporting Lisbon.

You see, they had this kid playing for them—a skinny, baby-faced seventeen-year-old with blond highlights in his hair.

This kid had everything. He had speed. He had vision. He had unbelievable skill. He left our defenders in the dust. He tormented Fabien. He performed astonishing tricks with the ball, then shrugged, as if to say, *Oh, that's nothing.*

Later, in the locker room, my teammates raved. Ronaldo, people said. Cristiano Ronaldo.

I stayed quiet, taking it all in—even the best players in the world were still capable of being awestruck.

Then I realized they weren't merely dazzled; they wanted him to play for us.

When Ferguson came into the locker room, several players rushed up to him.

"That kid, gaffer!" they exclaimed. *Gaffer* is the British term for boss. "We've got to sign that kid!"

Barely a week later, Ferguson announced that Cristiano Ronaldo had become a Manchester United player. He would wear the #7 shirt made famous by David Beckham.

We saw him. We wanted him. We got him.

One game, one glimpse of this Ronaldo, and suddenly we had the most promising young player any of us had ever seen.

That's just what life was like at Manchester United.

My new teammates were outstanding—better than anyone I'd ever played with. They were physically stronger. They were more advanced technically. They were faster in every way.

It's probably not an exaggeration to say that some of the balls they sent my way during training reached speeds greater than my old New Jersey car ever had.

I had to react more quickly, be more decisive.

Most of all, I had to win.

Winning was the only thing that mattered at Manchester United. Talent didn't matter. Potential didn't matter. If I was going to keep up with them—if I was going to stay on this team—I'd have to win.

Boy, it was a lot of pressure.

I called Kasey Keller, the US National Team goalkeeper, in London.

Kasey had been living in England, playing for various Premier League teams, for nine of the last eleven years.

"So . . . uh . . . what do I need to know?" I asked. It was a stupid question. But I didn't know how to express everything I felt. Overnight, I'd gone from MLS obscurity to this huge stage with its bright lights.

There were no words to describe how much pressure I felt.

I also didn't dare put into words the feeling that kept gnawing at me: *I'm not quite ready for this yet.*

Kasey thought for a while, then answered simply, "Well, Tim," he said, "I guess my advice to you would be this: try to make as many saves as you can."

In Europe, soccer seasons often open with a "Super Cup"—one champion playing another for best-of-the-best status.

In England, that super-championship is the Community Shield. There, the winner of the Premier League meets the winner of the FA Cup tournament.

Manchester United was the Premier League champion for the 2002–2003 season, which meant that we would face Arsenal, the FA Cup champion, just before the new season kicked off.

This was bound to be an exciting match. Arsenal, like Man U, was one of the great Premier League powers. The London club had many international stars. They had a quick passing game. They attacked with flair. They'd already won nine FA Cups and twelve First Division and Premier League titles.

Just hours before the game, Tony Coton told me I'd be the starting goalkeeper.

Not Fabien Barthez. Me.

Apparently I'd impressed Alex Ferguson in those preseason friendly games I'd played. Now he was shaking up the starting keeper position.

In the locker room, I saw a gray-and-white Manchester United goalkeeper's jersey on a hanger with my name on it.

I'll be wearing that today, I thought. *I'll be wearing that when I play for Manchester United.*

The game felt like war from the first whistle. We took the lead when Manchester United's Mikel Silvestre headed in a goal off a corner kick. Then Thierry Henry—Arsenal's all-time goal-scorer—won a free kick about thirty-five yards out.

With free kicks, the goalkeeper often sets up a defensive "wall"—a line of players who stand shoulder to shoulder. The wall closes off parts of the goal to the shooter.

As a keeper, I could choose how many players I wanted for the wall.

On the one hand, I wanted to cover as much of the goal as I could. On the other hand, I didn't want to block a clear view of the ball, or leave the Arsenal attackers unmarked.

I called for a three-man wall. I positioned myself in the unprotected area of the goal.

Thierry struck with power and precision. The ball flew over the wall I'd set up.

I dove. I stretched my body flat out. But I couldn't reach. The ball tucked inches inside the right post.

At halftime, Ferguson just about took my head off.

"A three-man wall!" he shouted at me. The muscles around his jaw were so tight I could see them flex.

"Against Henry! That's idiotic! You needed four men on that wall, Tim. You've got to think"—he jabbed both index fingers at his forehead—"when you play this game."

He was so angry that I saw the red veiny parts on the whites of his eyeballs. He went on and on. Then on some more.

I'd never had a coach scream at me like this. Not even Mulch!

The man scared the wits out of me.

"I'll send you right back to the MLS!" he shouted. I heard the disdain in his voice when he said MLS. As we headed for the locker room, he called after me.

"You're not in America anymore, son."

Neither team scored in the second half. When the final whistle blew, the match was deadlocked at 1–1.

There's no overtime in the Community Shield. The game would be settled by a penalty kick shoot-out.

I love penalty kick shoot-outs. I have loved them since I was twelve years old.

They're high pressure, and the likelihood of actually making a save is fairly low. But a keeper doesn't need to stop them all. If you can save one or two, you generally end up a hero.

PKs are decisive, too: just me vs. the shooter. There's a clear winner. The ball either goes in, or it doesn't. One team gets enough in and earns the win . . . or the other team does.

Most of the time, a penalty kick is a guessing game. Which way will the shooter kick? Which way should I dive?

If I can, I make an educated guess. Keepers spend a lot of time studying videos of different shooters' PK histories. I also try to read the shooter's body language, some tiny motion he makes in his run-up to the ball that hints at what kind of shot he might take.

More often than not, I have to make a wild guess.

Manchester United's Paul Scholes stepped up first. The Arsenal keeper danced all over the box. He sashayed back and forth, trying to distract Paul.

But Paul scored. One for our side.

Then I faced down the Brazilian player Edu. As he waited for the ref to blow the whistle, I cut quickly right, then left. I wanted to fake him out, put him out of his rhythm. It didn't work: his shot was beyond my reach. He scored.

1–1.

Our Rio Ferdinand scored. Then I stopped the next Arsenal shot.

2–1.

We missed the next shot. Arsenal made theirs.

2–2.

Man U: score.

Arsenal: score.

Man U: score.

Now we were up 4–3.

Arsenal's Robert Pirès stepped up. If he could make the shot, the game would keep going. If he missed—if I could stop it—Manchester United would win.

Pirès, who was French, had scored the winning goal in the FA Cup Final last year. He was generally regarded as one of the best players in the league.

It's a funny thing about Pirès. A few months before, I had watched the French national team on television. I happened to see Pirès take a penalty kick. For some reason, that image stuck in my head.

Standing now in the goal, with Pirès directly in front of me, I could picture the entire shot in my mind. I could see it. It was almost like I was watching a video replay. I remembered exactly how the ball veered sharply toward the low right corner of the goal.

I guessed that was what he would do again.

I had to extend my body fully, reach toward it with everything I had. But before I made contact with the ball, I knew: I had this one.

I forced it wide, knocked the ball to safety.

Instantly, half of the stadium—the roughly thirty thousand fans in Manchester United shirts—sprang to their feet. They cheered wildly.

And then there were those red shirts on the field: my teammates. They were flying at me in celebration. All those greats, wrapping their arms around me, playfully punching my stomach and rubbing my bald head. We'd won. We'd won on penalty kicks.

Just like that, I was a hero. I was one of them.

I glanced at the side of the field and saw Sir Alex Ferguson. He had a huge grin plastered across his face. He looked as if he had forgotten, by now, all about that "idiotic" three-man wall.

After that victory, Manchester United made me their starting keeper. They began to negotiate Fabien Barthez's transfer to a French team, Marseille.

It happened so fast.

I was proud to be the starting goalkeeper, but it also added to the pressure I felt. I knew that if I didn't play well, there would be somebody right behind me. Somebody who would be thrilled to jump into my place.

Fabien was a class act about the switch. He remained friendly toward me. Publicly, he made statements like, *I blame only myself if I lose my spot.* This from a guy who had won the Premier League the previous season, and who had won the World Cup and European Championship with France. Now he was watching as his job was handed to a twenty-four-year-old straight from the MLS.

In the most competitive position on the world's most competitive team, he was nothing but gracious.

If that should happen to me someday, I thought, *I hope I'd handle it the same way.*

* * *

Laura and I did our best to try to acclimate to life in Manchester.

First, we got a dog. Clayton was a goofy puppy who flopped all over the house, always getting in trouble.

If he didn't get a ton of exercise (and even sometimes when he did), Clayton started chewing the furniture or scratching at the doors. He knocked things over as he barreled through the house. He created chaos everywhere he went. Frankly, he reminded me of myself—the way my brother and I had run wildly all over Mom's apartment back in New Jersey.

But now it was my house; I suddenly understood my mom's exasperation.

"He's going to destroy this place!" I'd exclaim. Then I'd try to scold Clayton, and Laura would swoop him up. She'd pet behind his ears and say, "Aw, but he's just learning. And he's such a good boy.

"Aren't you a good boy, Clayton?" When she set him down, that dog would go bounding around the house to cause more trouble.

Clayton took forever to housebreak. When we came home from the grocery store, we might return to piles and puddles staining the hardwood floors. We'd stand in the doorway, temporarily frozen by the mess.

Then Laura would go into action mode. "You get the paper towels," she would say. "I'll get the plastic bag."

I played well. In my first nine games, I posted six clean sheets and had allowed just three goals. By January of 2004, I'd started in twenty-nine matches, posting a 22–5–2 record (twenty-two wins, five losses, two draws) . . . and fourteen shutouts.

The tabloids turned around their screaming head-lines pretty quickly.

The best-selling *Sun* noted, "This Yank's No Plank."

The *Express* agreed: "Yankee Doing Dandy."

Again and again, I was compared to the great Man-chester United goalkeeper, Peter Schmeichel. Both fans and experts ranked Schmeichel among the great goal-keepers in history. During one interview, Tony Coton said he believed that I could be even better than Schmeichel.

It was flattering. But every time I heard someone say this kind of thing, I wanted to say, *Wait. Please wait.*

I'd spent my entire life comparing myself to others.

First, I'd compared myself to the older boys in North-wood Estates.

Then I'd compared myself to the other players on the Youth National Team.

Next I'd compared myself to Tony Meola. Then Kasey Keller.

So I knew exactly how I stacked up against Schmeichel. I had talent, I had skill, I had drive, and a heck of a lot of potential. But I was no Schmeichel, not yet. I wasn't the best by a long shot, and I knew it.

I knew something else, too. As hard as I was working, and as lucky as I'd gotten, it was just a matter of time before I made a mistake. A big one.

CHAPTER 11
THE LONGEST SEASON

WINTERS IN MANCHESTER ARE LONG. THEY'RE MISERABLE.
By early September, the average daytime temperature is
in the fifties. It often dips to near freezing at night. Manchester sits as far north as many parts of Alaska, so as the
months go on, it starts getting dark by three p.m. Shops
are closed by five p.m.

And there's the rain.

The rain doesn't stop. There's a constant thin, cold
drizzle, and the dampness seeps into your bones. Not
long ago, a Manchester resident tracked the weather for
an entire year. He found that rainy days outnumbered
dry ones 198 to 167.

My training schedule was grueling. During the week I was so wiped from practice that all I could do was stumble home to take a nap.

I was even more tired after games—sometimes so sore and bruised it hurt to move.

My favorite part of each day came after my naps. That's when Laura and I took Clayton for long walks. We strolled over to a park, where Clayton romped with his canine playmates. He splashed along the river banks, and he peed on every available tree.

I loved that dog. I loved that he didn't know anything about goals or games. I loved that he wasn't impressed when he heard people whisper *Tim Howard . . . Manchester United . . . yeah, that's him.*

Most of all, I loved the way Laura looked at Clayton Her eyes went soft when she saw him. All he had to do was start thumping his tail on the floor, or twitch his legs in a dream, and she'd start cooing at him. And when I was anxious before a game—or disappointed after one—Clayton could always break through the stress. He could always make me laugh.

Laura missed home. She'd grown up in the midst of a huge southern family. Until we got married she lived within a few miles of two dozen cousins. Now the only regular contact she had with any of them was via overseas phone calls or the occasional visit.

She missed smaller comforts, too. Soon after we'd moved to Manchester, she ordered a salad in a restaurant. She'd expected the kind of thing she would have gotten at home—a full meal in a bowl with chopped vegetables and nuts and dried fruits with a good dressing.

Or at least some dressing.

Instead she got a sad plate of dry lettuce leaves.

She didn't complain—Laura was trying to be positive, to treat this relocation like an adventure. But I saw her eyes welling with tears.

"Laura?" I asked. "Are you okay?"

Her face crumpled. Lettuce leaves still in her mouth, she began to cry in earnest.

"I just want to go to Chili's," she said. She closed her eyes, tried to chew, but tears were pouring down her face. "I want to be at Chili's, and I want my family, and I want it to be warm outside, and I want to have a decent salad."

And then she was laughing and crying all at once. Laughing, because she knew how ridiculous it sounded to cry over a bad salad while yearning for Chili's.

Crying, because she really was yearning. She was yearning for salads and Chili's and everything else about home.

* * *

I often lingered after practice to hone my skills. But no matter how much extra time I spent practicing, I was never the last to leave the field. That's because no one could outwork Cristiano Ronaldo.

Cristiano has always had plenty of flash. Today people say he's arrogant, that he's all about glitz and glamour. But what I remember is how hard he trained.

Long after everyone else left the field, Cristiano was still out there. He'd run around the perimeter of the training grounds, working on his ball skills. He did it in the rain. He did it in the sleet. He did it in the snow.

I remember watching him one afternoon as the rain pelted down.

That guy's going to be the best in the world, I thought.

He did a lightning fast step-over, without breaking stride.

If he isn't already.

By March, I'd been playing high-intensity soccer for fourteen months straight.

I'd gone from the MLS preseason in January 2003 to the regular season. From there I'd gone straight into the Premier League season.

Even the holidays had offered no respite. I trained on Christmas morning, then played a game the very next day.

I was so tired by now. I desperately needed a break.

But Manchester United's season wouldn't finish until the very end of May. I had three more months of nonstop competition.

I'd never faced stakes this high, for this long, at this level of intensity.

When you win, you don't question it. You don't wonder how you pulled off that save. You don't wonder why you happened to play well.

It's only when you lose that the self-examination begins.

I can pinpoint the day it started for me: March 9, 2004.

The best teams in Europe compete in a tournament called the UEFA Champions League tournament. It is the most important international club competition.

Earlier in the season, we'd played six Champions League games. We won five, and we advanced to the knockout stage.

Now, we'd meet FC Porto, a club in the top league of Portuguese soccer.

After playing them, both home and away, the team with the highest aggregate score—the combined score from both games—would advance to the quarterfinals. If we had the same total goals, whichever of us had the most away goals (which count for more than home goals) would be the winner.

We expected to win. Easily.

But the first game, played at Porto, didn't go as planned. Although we took an early lead, they played intensely. Porto's striker, Benni McCarthy, sent two brilliant goals right past me. We lost 2–1.

In the second game, we took the lead in the thirty-second minute. All we had to do was hold that line. If the score remained 1–0, our aggregate score would be tied. We'd have two goals in two games, and they'd have two goals in two games.

The away-goal rule would give us the advantage, and we'd win.

With two minutes left in injury time, Porto earned a free kick. Benni McCarthy—the guy who scored on me twice in the last game—would take it.

I organized the wall of defense. McCarthy struck. The ball flew past the line of defenders. It curled toward the net.

I've replayed that moment a thousand times since. I know exactly what I did wrong. I had two options: catch the ball, or parry it into a safe area beyond the box. A truly top keeper, an experienced keeper, would have had the confidence to do one or the other.

Today, I'd have that confidence. A decade ago, though, I was still raw.

I got my hands on the ball. I even knocked it away

from the goal. But I made a huge mistake when I did that. I didn't send it to the right place.

I sent it back into the danger zone. Smack-dab in front of the six-yard box.

Porto's Francisco Costinha pounced on the rebound. His shot came sailing toward my right.

I dove. I stretched. I extended my hands toward the ball as far as I possibly could. It's possible the tips of my gloves even grazed the ball. But this time I missed.

The ball slid into the far corner of the net.

And just like that, Porto had equalized the game—enough to earn them a win on aggregate scores.

Before I even hit the ground, I understood: we were out of the Champions League.

Porto went on to win that year's Champions League title. In time their coach, Jose Mourinho, would be considered one of the greatest coaches in all of soccer.

We were knocked out of the Champions League when we should have gotten through.

And it was my fault.

I was numb. As the game ended, I moved past my teammates, shook hands with the Porto players, and left the field as soon as possible. I headed down the tunnel toward the locker room. All the while, I kept hearing this voice in my head: *You lost this.*

You did this. You lost.

Behind that refrain, I felt a storm brewing.

Somehow, I knew that everything was about to change.

CHAPTER 12
BENCHED

I TOOK THE BLAME FOR THAT CHAMPIONS LEAGUE LOSS—IN the papers, among the fans, with Ferguson, and with my teammates. But nobody criticized me more than I criticized myself.

Stopping that ball was my job. It was the job I signed up for when I came to Man U. I'd failed.

My old coach Mulch called me from the United States. He was the goalkeeping coach for the Kansas City Wizards now. He had caught the last five minutes of the game. I knew his heart must have sunk down to his toes when he learned what I'd done.

"Listen, Tim," he said. "You'll have other games. You'll have other saves."

I thanked him, but it didn't matter.

That voice inside me wasn't going to stop.

Everyone had been calling me the next Peter Schmeichel, but I knew I wasn't there yet.

I could be someday. I swear I could be, but I was still young, still learning.

I needed time.

But time was a luxury I wouldn't get at Manchester United.

Five days after Porto, we played our crosstown rivals, Manchester City. We lost badly: 4–1. After that, Alex Ferguson announced that our backup keeper, Roy Carroll, would be playing in the next three games.

It meant I'd be on the bench for our second Premier League match against Arsenal.

"That's ridiculous," said Laura when I told her. She had fire in her eyes. "We're talking about one mistake, Tim."

I shrugged. "Yeah, well . . ."

She stood there, waiting for the end of that sentence.

"It was a really big mistake," I said.

* * *

I'm sure if I'd come onto the team as the backup keeper, like I'd expected, it wouldn't have hurt so much.

But I'd had such a glorious start. It felt terrible.

Ferguson put me back in for the final month of the season. Something had changed, though. I could feel it.

I could feel it in the way Tony Coton spoke to me during practice—or rather didn't. We went through our routines—our high volleys and low balls. Sometimes, if he didn't like how I went after one, he'd snap at me. Beyond that, though, I got very little feedback.

After training, he'd just disappear, scurrying off the field, almost as if he didn't want to be seen with me.

Or like he'd given up on me.

Because of my TS, I clear my throat a lot. I do it more when I'm excited or nervous. Which means I clear my throat a *lot* before games. The closer to kickoff, the more I do it.

Before one of the final games of the season, my phone rang. It was my agent, Dan.

"You okay?" he asked.

"Yeah, why?"

There was a pause. "Well, I got a call from Tony Coton. He said you're throwing up in the bathroom."

I scratched my head. Had Coton heard my throat

clearing and mistaken the sound of it for throwing up?

There was a long pause, and Dan added, "Tony's asking a lot of questions about your Tourette Syndrome."

I felt my jaw harden. "Why?"

"He seems to think it's affecting your play."

My TS had never been an issue in terms of my goalkeeping. Never. Not here, not at the MetroStars, not on the Imperials. Not even as a kid.

Suddenly I felt like I was back in school, like I had to hide my condition again.

"You tell him he has nothing to worry about," I muttered into the phone.

Leaving Old Trafford that day, I kept my eyes fixed ahead. If Tony Coton or Alex Ferguson were anywhere in the vicinity, I didn't want to run into them.

I didn't even want to look at them.

At the very end of the season, Tony Coton approached me before practice.

He told me I'd won the Professional Footballers' Association Goalkeeper of the Year award—the most prestigious award in England.

He said it in such a matter-of-fact manner. It took a moment to sink in.

When it finally registered, my jaw just about fell open.

Each year, the PFA awards are given at an invitation-only gala dinner. The event is held in London. It's like Oscars night for the Premier League. There are limos. A red carpet. Tuxedos. Paparazzi.

It's not the kind of event you miss. If you're one of the eleven men to earn an award for your position, you go. Which is why it was so strange that Tony didn't say a word about the event. He simply informed me I was getting the award, and then—bizarrely—he walked away.

A few months ago, Coton had paraded me around and patted himself on the back for discovering me. Now, it was like he was embarrassed at the idea that I might represent Manchester United at the awards banquet.

The event came and went, and neither of us spoke of it again. A trophy arrived later in the mail. It was a shiny symbol of someplace I'd never been.

Laura and I went home to Memphis at the end of that season. We'd had a house built there during our year in England, and we were thrilled to spend the summer lying by the pool. I spent a lot of time with the US National Team. Then, in the blink of an eye, summer was over.

I returned to England with a feeling of dread.

Roy Carroll and I spent the 2004–2005 season playing goalkeeping musical chairs. Roy was their first choice for a while. Then, when he made a mistake, they put me in the game. I lasted until my next error. Then I was out, and Roy was back in.

And I did make errors. Many of them now.

I'd started playing too cautiously.

I knew I was on a short rope—a very short rope. I knew that everything I did was going to be scrutinized in a way it never had been before.

My game changed.

I focused more on avoiding mistakes than on winning games. I kept thinking, *Just get through this game. Make sure that if a goal does go in, it's not your fault.*

As long as it wasn't my fault, I figured, I could stay on the team.

It was the worst possible mind-set a keeper can have. A keeper needs to do everything in his power to stop the ball. Period.

In one game, I punched a ball out of the box. It was a weaker punch than I'd intended, and my teammate Rio Ferdinand scolded me, "Tim, you've got to catch the ball."

So the next time the ball came toward me, in the same game, I caught it. But the catch was loose, just barely in my arms. Roy Keane looked at me ferociously. "Punch that thing," Roy said. His voice was laced with venom. "Punch it next time, okay?"

I thought about Kasey Keller. I thought about how

relaxed he always looked out there in the goal. He seemed so confident. He had courage and conviction when he stood in goal.

I didn't. Not anymore. Now I was afraid to take any risk at all.

The fans sure noticed, every bit as much as my teammates and coaches. One afternoon, a little old lady followed me around the grocery store. She was almost as old as my nana back home. And I'm telling you: she glared at me. There she was in the dairy section as I put milk in the cart. Then again by the breads. The bottled water.

Each time I saw her, I walked away. Then she'd emerge around a corner in another aisle, her eyes fixed on me like daggers.

Finally, in the produce section, I looked right at her.

"Hi," I said. "How are you?"

She glowered at me. "Well, I'd be doing a lot better," she said, "if you boys could start winning for a change."

Around that time, my mom visited. She bustled around the kitchen, filling our house with the smell of Hungarian food.

I was so stressed out by this point that I could barely

talk to her. I left for practice in the morning. Came home. Napped. I felt her watching me, and I recognized the look on her face: it was the same look she'd had back when I was a kid and I touched her on the shoulder before talking to her. It was a look of deep worry.

When the two of us were alone, Mom said, "Can I ask you something?"

"Sure."

"Do you still love soccer?"

I didn't even have to think about my answer.

"No," I said. "I don't."

Looking back, I'll bet she already knew the answer before she asked the question. She probably wanted to make sure I knew the answer, too.

By now, I was calling Mulch to ask him what he saw in my games. Since I wasn't getting any feedback from Coton, Mulch became my go-to guy.

He faithfully watched every game, and he was completely honest.

"You're not playing like yourself," he said. "You're stiff. Your face is tight. You look like you're not enjoying yourself."

He was right; I hated playing small like that. I hated how it felt to be afraid.

The season dragged.

Then one day in the spring, the doorbell rang. I opened the door. I couldn't believe my eyes.

It was Mulch! My New Jersey coach, standing right on my doorstep in England. I stood there gaping at him for a few long moments before inviting him in.

Laura had flown him over as a surprise. And what a great surprise it was!

We spent a long time talking about my game, about what had gone wrong.

Mulch's advice was simple: "Just be Tim Howard," he said. "If you can get back to doing what you do, you'll be fine."

Then Laura and I got good news . . . the very best kind of news. We were going to have a baby.

In that one moment, I forgot all about my professional slump. Just for that one moment, everything in the world was as good as it gets.

At the end of that season, we met Arsenal again in the FA Cup Final. Roy Carroll played, and I watched from the sidelines.

By the end of ninety minutes, the game was tied, 0–0.

We went into extra time, and still no goals. After a

while, it seemed clear: we were headed for a penalty kick shoot-out.

Ferguson turned around. "Tim," he said. "Go warm up."

Good, I thought. *He's going to put me in for the penalty kick shoot-out. I'm good at penalty kick shoot-outs. I'm going to win this game for the team.*

Everything is about to turn around, I thought.

I warmed up, then went back to the bench. I waited. The clock ticked by. Players ran up and down the field.

I stood again, jogged up and down the field. I stretched. I wanted to stay fresh.

"Why are you warming up, Tim?" someone asked.

"He's going to put me in for the shoot-out," I said.

I sat back down. I watched the back of Ferguson's head. Any minute, he was going to turn around and send me in.

The whistle blew, and the teams started toward the goal for the shoot-out.

Ferguson didn't turn around. He didn't say a word. He just sat there watching as Roy Carroll walked toward the goal.

Let me in, I wanted to scream. *I'm right here, and I can do this. I can handle penalty kick shoot-outs like no one else I know.*

I didn't say anything, though. I never went in. We lost that shoot-out, lost the game.

Manchester United finished the season third in the league. It was only the fourth season in sixteen years that we hadn't earned a league trophy.

In June, Laura and I returned to Memphis—back to our house, back to her family, back to our life there. We sat by the pool and watched her belly grow. We talked endlessly about the baby that was on its way.

Not long after we'd returned, my phone rang. Alex Ferguson was on the other end of the line. You know something's up when your English coach calls you during the off-season, from another continent.

"Did Tony tell you?" he asked.

"Tell me what?" Tony hadn't talked to me since the season ended.

"We're releasing Roy Carroll. We've signed Edwin van der Sar."

Van der Sar was Dutch. He played on another Premier League team. He was good.

No. He was better than good. He was great.

"You should know that nothing's set in stone," said Ferguson. "The first keeper job's still up for grabs."

He was reassuring me, but I didn't buy it. Sometimes a team's actions say it all. If it hadn't been obvious from my back-and-forth with Carroll, it sure was now: Manchester United didn't believe in me anymore.

In a few months, I'd have a child. I didn't want my kid to see me sitting on the bench, earning a paycheck for watching others play. I didn't want him to watch my potential withering on the vine.

I wanted to play.

CHAPTER 13
#24

AS EXPECTED, EDWIN WAS THE FIRST KEEPER FROM THE
start. Tony Coton fawned over him the way he'd once
fawned over me.

Edwin wasn't a bad guy. He was a gentleman, in fact.
He was always polite, always decent. And he was a heck
of a keeper. He had reach and precision. He also had an
uncanny instinct for anticipating where the ball would
land. At six foot six, he could stretch so far in goal that he
made near-impossible shots look easy. He was also wonderfully clear with the defenders.

But Edwin was focused on his own game. He wasn't
going to mentor me, or anybody else.

But I can learn from Edwin by watching, I thought. *If I don't let my ego get in the way. If I don't let my feelings be hurt, Edwin can help make me better.*

The best day of my life? Not even a question: September 5, 2005. That's when I became a father.

Jacob. Sweet Jacob, my son. He was born in a hospital in Manchester. The day he was born, I stared down at his perfect face, his tiny lashes, the delicate curve of his nose. I felt my heart, my whole world, crack wide open.

Moments after I held him for the first time, I walked out to the waiting room. My mom and Laura's mom sat together. They looked up hopefully. Nervously.

"It's a boy," I announced proudly. Later, my mom would tell me that I was wearing the biggest grin she'd ever seen on me in my whole life. "His name is Jacob."

In an instant, they were out of their seats, hugging and kissing me.

"How can you be a father?" my mother said. She planted a kiss on my cheek. I felt wet tears on my skin. "How can you possibly be a father, when I can still remember holding you?"

The nurses sent me home by seven p.m. Laura insisted I bring one of the blankets that Jacob had been wrapped in.

"Show it to Clayton," Laura had said. "Let him smell

it so he gets used to the baby."

I tried, but Clayton gave that thing one sniff before walking away.

Nope, he seemed to be saying. *Not interested.*

Clayton was the only one who didn't adore Jacob from the start. When we brought the baby home, Clayton sniffed him, curious about this new plaything. But when Jacob didn't play back, Clayton took offense.

From then on, if Clayton was lounging on the sofa and we sat down with Jacob in our arms, Clayton would coolly get off the couch and head to a far corner of the room. He'd sulk at us, as if saying, *Make your choice, people: it's going to be me, or that baby.*

"Well, it's not going to be you, Clayton," I'd grumble.

Laura would lean over and scratch that hound's ears.

"Be nice to Clayton," she said. "His whole world just got turned upside down."

I watched Edwin all season. I made mental notes.

I watched the way he moved—how he caught the ball. How he punched. Most of all, I observed his confidence. And I learned.

I sat on the bench.

Some keepers would surely have been happy to remain the Man U backup. After all, there's great money. You get royal treatment, even as a backup.

And just like a backup quarterback in American football, the backup keeper is rarely used . . . so I could have money and status without tremendous day-in-day-out pressure.

Still, now that Edwin was here, I heard a constant voice in my head: *You can do better than sitting on the bench. You can be great. Go somewhere that you can become the best.*

Go somewhere that you can play.

I lasted the rest of that season. But I told Manchester United that I wanted to go on loan to another team—somewhere I'd be a first keeper.

I learned that Everton Football Club was looking for a starting keeper.

Everton was another Premier League team, based in Liverpool. They played in a great old-time stadium, Goodison Park. It was rickety, with mismatched beams. I'd always loved the feel of the place. It was authentic.

The morning after a home game, I went to the Everton training ground. The Everton coach, David Moyes, was waiting.

Moyes was a tall guy, very lanky. He was younger than Ferguson. He had red hair, a firm jaw, striking pale-blue eyes. He had scars above his eyebrows—reminders of wounds from his own days on the field.

He cut to the chase. "I think we could use a keeper like you."

Everton, he said, wasn't big and wealthy like Manchester United. They didn't have the massive budgets to buy any player they wanted. They had only a fraction of the staff that Man U had. They didn't have the worldwide attention, or the same level of corporate sponsorships.

Or, frankly, the winning record.

But they had history. They'd competed at the top of English soccer for over a hundred seasons. And Moyes had big plans for the team.

"We're ambitious," he said. "And I know you're ambitious, too."

Moyes also said that there weren't a lot of big egos on the team. That it was a real family club. A great playing environment.

He's selling me on the place, I thought. *He's selling me, because he wants me on the team.*

And that felt amazing—to be wanted again. I'd felt so disposable at Manchester United, for so long.

I asked the most important question of all: "And what if I have a bad game?"

He didn't even blink. "Tim, you're young. I want you to learn," he said. "Learning requires risk, so I'm going to encourage you to take risks. Sometimes you'll make mistakes. When you do, I'm going to be straight with you.

I'm going to be honest. I might even scream and holler from time to time. But I'm not going to take you out of the game. Ultimately, I believe you'll win us more games than you'll lose us."

I'm not going to take you out of the game.

In that moment, it was as if somebody had opened up a window for me and let in a blast of fresh air.

Everton and Manchester United worked out a loan agreement: I'd still officially be an employee of Manchester United. But I'd play for Everton the next season. I'd train with Everton, I'd play in their games. At the end of the season, we'd reevaluate.

About a week later, Everton called to ask what number I wanted to wear.

Call it OCD, or call it a personality quirk, but I've always liked even numbers better than odd. I like twos and fours best of all.

"Number 24," I said. "I want 24."

Laura ordered an Everton jersey in Jacob's size. It was a special order—the back said HOWARD above the number 24.

The morning I left for my final Manchester United game, Jacob was crawling around the house in that Everton jersey, the number 24 on his tiny back.

I scooped him up. "Looks good on you, little man." I

kissed his cheek, his neck, the top of his head.

Then set him down and walked out the door, headed to my final day on the Manchester United bench.

My deal with Everton was just a loan; there was no guarantee of anything. It was possible that after a year with Everton, I'd head right back to Manchester United's bench.

But that's not what I believed.

From that meeting with David Moyes, I believed I'd be at Everton for a long, long time.

CHAPTER 14
LIKE COMING HOME

ON SATURDAYS, THE EVERTON FANS COME STREAMING toward Goodison Park. They form a parade of bright blue: blue scarves, blue hats, blue jerseys, blue jackets. When they enter the stadium, they take their seats in bright-blue stadium chairs.

"Come on, Blue Boys!" they shout to us as we play.

They're loud, and they're rowdy. I believe they're some of the greatest fans on earth.

I loved Everton from the first game I played. It was August 19, 2006, and we enjoyed a nail-biter of a win against Watford.

Watford's keeper that day was Ben Foster. Foster,

weirdly, was also a Manchester United goalkeeper, also out on loan. When Foster had signed for Man U, he'd announced that he was coming to take my job.

Then Van der Sar arrived and took both our jobs.

What a strange world this is, I thought, *that both goalkeepers on the field are Manchester United keepers, both playing for other teams.*

I didn't know what Foster's loan experience was like, but I'd been welcomed at Everton with open arms. By the fans, by my teammates, by all the staff, by David Moyes.

I adored my new goalkeeping coach, Chris Woods. On our very first day of training together, Chris set up a bunch of drills.

Then he added, "If you feel like you need something specific, something I'm not doing, let me know. I'll do whatever you need to help you be ready."

I'll do whatever you need to help you be ready.

Those were words I never heard at Manchester United. Not once. Not when I was playing well, not when I was playing poorly.

I've since played with Chris for hundreds and hundreds of games—at Everton, and later, too, on the US Men's National Team.

In all those years, his confidence in me—his willingness to help me exactly as I needed it—has never wavered.

Every single game, win or lose, Chris shakes my hand, pats me on the back.

Then we get back to work.

Liverpool is a port city. It's built on the banks of the River Mersey. The people who live there—nicknamed "Scousers," after the traditional stew—are the dockworkers, the steelworkers. They are hardworking people, fierce in their loyalties.

And their loyalties are divided between two teams: Everton and the Liverpool Football Club. The two might play in stadiums less than a mile apart, but they are archrivals.

The Merseyside rivalry pits neighbor against neighbor, family member against family member. Driving through Liverpool's streets, you'll see blue Everton flags hanging mere feet from red Liverpool ones. Inside those homes, half the household might wear blue, the other half red.

That's the thing: Scousers are blue or they're red. They're Everton or Liverpool. Period.

They're so passionate about their respective teams that the trash bins in the city of Liverpool can't be either red or blue. The trash bins are all purple.

Twice a year, Everton and Liverpool meet on the

field—once at Goodison Park, and once at Anfield, Liverpool's home stadium. Those games are called the derby (pronounced "darby"). While there are plenty of other derbies in the Premier League—Arsenal vs. Tottenham, for example, or Manchester United vs. Manchester City—the Merseyside derby is the most intense rivalry of all.

My fourth game with Everton, September 9, 2006, would be my first Merseyside derby.

As the game drew closer, people shouted to me from the streets.

People in blue shouted, "You beat those Reds this weekend!"

People dressed in red shouted . . . well . . . those Liverpool fans shouted different things entirely.

In the days before the derby, the Everton halls buzzed with excitement. Not just the players, either. The cooks in the kitchen, all the support staff. Everyone was excited about this game.

"You make sure you get those Reds!" a laundry woman called to me as we passed in the hallway.

"Gonna take 'em down, are ya?" said another woman who cleared my plate after a team breakfast.

Jimmy Martin, Everton's cranky old "kit man"—the guy who's in charge of all the uniforms and warm-up gear—regaled me with stories of past derbies. Then he narrowed his eyes. "I know you're on loan," he said, "but you're going to play the game like a true Blue, aren't 'cha?"

"Yeah, Jimmy," I answered. "I sure am."

And I meant it.

There's a lot to remember about that first Merseyside derby.

I remember, for example, the moments before the game. I remember the flood of pride I felt when "Theme from Z-Cars," the Everton fight song, started up. I remember hearing the crowd go wild when the music started.

As we walked out to the field, all the other Everton players touched a sign that said HOME OF THE BLUES.

I didn't touch it, though. I was just on loan, and I hadn't earned that honor. Not yet.

What I remember most are the Everton fans. They were raucous and passionate in all the right ways. I saw them leaping out of their seats again and again. With each roar they told us that they had our backs. They reminded me, in many ways, of my own family: hardworking, determined, and hopeful.

When I was a kid, I wanted to score goals to make my mom happy.

Now, as an adult, I wanted to make saves to make these fans happy.

I made my first save in the first seconds of the game. Then I made every one after that. We crushed Liverpool that day; we won the game 3–0. It was Everton's biggest victory over the crosstown rivals in forty-two years.

The crowd went absolutely bonkers. They sang and hugged and leaped and wept.

Later that afternoon, I was back at home with Laura and Jacob. Jacob and I were playing peekaboo. Every time I pulled my hands away from my face and cried, "Peeka-boo!" he burst into giggles.

"You know what, Tim?" Laura said. "You haven't once wondered what David Moyes thinks about you."

"That's because I'm not worried," I said.

Jacob kicked out his chubby feet, so I did another peekaboo.

It was true. I didn't feel insecure around Moyes. Sure, I'd noticed him during the derby. I'd hugged him proudly at the end of it.

But I hadn't been concerned about what he thought of my performance. For me, the game had been all about those fans.

I smiled at Jacob. "Your daddy's a Blue Boy," I said. "Your daddy plays for Everton."

* * *

I started to develop some pregame rituals.

The line between superstition and preparation—maybe even superstition and OCD—can be very blurry. But the things I did before those early Everton games felt right.

So I did them the next time. And the time after that. I've done them ever since.

For example, I didn't touch the Everton sign in the tunnel. I have never touched it since. Hundreds and hundreds of games later, I still won't do it.

Superstition? Probably. But somehow not touching it helps me *feel* ready. And if it makes me feel ready, it makes me ready. When I taped my hands for those early games, I did it in a specific order. It's the same way I do it today.

My own rituals quickly blended with my teammates'.

When Leon Osman and I shook hands before an early game, we bumped shoulders. Years later, if we don't follow the handshake with a shoulder tap—if our shoulders don't make contact—I'll say, "That doesn't feel right."

And Leon will agree. "Let's do it again."

Sometimes I drove the staff crazy with my rituals, too.

Before games, Jimmy Martin set out my warm-up

clothes. At six foot three, I'm a size large, so that's what he set out: large.

But one day I put on my warm-up clothes, and they felt . . . wrong. Wrong in the same way that packing my bags before youth league games in New Jersey felt wrong.

Wrong like, it had to be changed right now.

I sent for Jimmy, and he came in grumbling.

"I need a medium," I said.

He looked confused. "But you're a large, Tim."

I shook my head. "I need a medium today, Jimmy."

Soon, that became another pregame ritual: trying on different sizes. Sometimes a large felt right, and sometimes a medium felt right.

It didn't take long for Jimmy to start setting out two complete outfits, one in each size.

The Everton players had their own rituals, too. I learned pretty quickly that you don't close the door to the bathroom stall. Ever. Not even when you need to—how shall I put this?—sit down.

Mind you, these bathrooms are tiny. When you're sitting on the toilet with the door open, everyone sees you going to the bathroom. Even the coach.

If Moyes walked in while I sat on the pot, pants at my ankles, I'd shrug, like, *Yeah, I know this is weird, but what can you do?*

Moyes shook his head and averted his eyes, just as he did for every player. *Whatever,* he seemed to be saying. Whatever we needed to do to feel prepared out there.

At Christmas, I joined the Everton team for their annual hospital visit. There, the Everton Santa Claus—dressed only in blue and white, because red belongs to that other Liverpool team—delivered gifts to children.

One of our defenders, Alan Stubbs, walked over to me. He placed his hand on my back. "Tim," he said, "I wanted to tell you that you've done brilliant for us so far."

I was about to say thanks, but he held up his hand.

"Don't get me wrong," he added. "You've got a long way to go. But the fans have really taken a liking to you. It feels . . ."

He paused for a moment. "Feels like you've become one of us, really."

I said only one word, "Thanks." Inside, though, I swelled with pride.

Alan shrugged. "Don't let it go to your head, mate."

Moyes was true to his word with me. Even when I had a bad game, he put me right back in the next one . . . and in the three hundred games after that.

He let me make mistakes, then learn from them.

* * *

We'd go on that season to finish in sixth place. In the spring, David Moyes made me a permanent offer, for more money than I'd ever earned at Manchester United.

I felt like I'd hit the jackpot in every way. Bigger salary. Supportive teammates. A goalkeeping coach whom I trusted completely. A head coach who trusted *me* completely. The confidence that I could keep playing no matter what.

All I needed was to shake the feeling that had welled up during my time at Manchester United: the feeling that somehow I wasn't good enough.

CHAPTER 15
SLAYING THE DRAGON

LAURA AND I HAD A SECOND CHILD IN 2007, AT THE END OF MY first season with Everton. Alivia—we called her Ali— made a dramatic entrance into this world. She didn't make a peep for the first five seconds of her life.

It was only seconds, but when you are waiting to hear your baby's first cry, five seconds can seem like an eternity.

Laura and I glanced at each other nervously. We waited. Still no sound. Then, just when our anxiety hit full-blown panic, the baby girl let loose with an earsplitting wail. It was like she was saying, *Yeah, I'm here, all right, and I mean it.*

141

Already, we could tell she was a force to be reckoned with.

Right from the start, Ali had strong opinions. She fidgeted and fussed, struggled to sleep, could switch from laughter to howling in an instant. A person never had to wonder whether Ali was happy or sad. Whatever she was, you couldn't help but know.

But man, that girl could light up a room. Her energy was dazzling.

By spring of 2009, Ali was two years old, and Jacob was four.

Everything was good. Better than good.

It was my third year at Everton. We had a strong defense by now. We had excellent communication on the field, and we trusted one another. Walking into each game, it felt like we stood a good chance, genuinely, of earning a clean sheet. By May, I would have the most number of clean sheets, seventeen, in one season in all of Everton's hundred-year history.

I had a great rhythm down: I trained hard all week, then played hard on Saturdays.

Then I devoted my Sundays to my family. The four of us often went to Tatton Park, a thousand-acre park with lush gardens and a painted carousel and a working farm. A miniature train ran through the park, pulled slowly along by a tractor. We'd step into a train car, and that little tractor would pull us to the barn. There, the kids fed gentle pigs and goats and cows. They were mesmerized by the animals.

It was a happy time for me, both personally and professionally.

Sometimes I thought about Manchester United and wondered why I'd doubted myself so much. Other times, when I thought about them, I felt those old pangs—those feelings of not having been wanted. I wondered how long those feelings would stick with me.

That year, we started our run for the FA Cup with a game against a lower-league team called Macclesfield. We would play on their turf: the tiny Moss Rose Stadium, where Macclesfield has played for over a hundred years.

When I say tiny, I mean tiny.

We were accustomed to playing in Premier League stadiums that hold sixty thousand or more. But the total capacity of Moss Rose, including standing room, was one-tenth of that.

As for seats, there were only 2,600 of those—barely more than my high school gymnasium.

The Macclesfield locker rooms were so small and cluttered that players had to make a choice. We could either sit on the bench, or we could put our bag on it. We couldn't do both.

David Moyes didn't want us to be distracted by the snug conditions. So the day before the game, he took us to Moss Rose Stadium to check it out.

It had been snowing and sleeting for days. This tiny little stadium had no high-tech drainage or heating system (by contrast, Manchester United had recently installed a multimillion-dollar field, complete with twenty-three miles of heating pipes below the turf).

To protect the grass, the team had covered the field with tarps. They'd weighed down the tarps with sandbags. Now, the day before the game, they had to remove the tarps, as well as the snow and sleet that had piled on top.

Who did this team get to help them? Their fans.

The field was overflowing with fans. They were slogging around in the sleet, shoveling snow, doing everything necessary to make sure the game could be played. It reminded me of my old Imperials days—having to clear away the geese before we could kick a ball.

I loved seeing this. I loved the reminder of how passionate soccer fans are, all around the world.

Thanks to the fans' efforts, the game went on the next day. Macclesfield fought hard. And although we beat them, 1–0, they earned our endless respect with their phenomenal team spirit, both the players' and fans' alike.

After that, in our FA Cup run, we faced only Premier League teams—and some mighty good ones, too.

We tied Liverpool in the fourth round, then beat them 1–0 in a replay.

We defeated Aston Villa next, winning comfortably, 3–1.

In the quarters we knocked off Middlesbrough 2–1 to advance to the semifinals.

There, in the semifinals, we'd meet none other than Manchester United. My old team.

It's hard to describe just how high the stakes felt before the Man U match. If we could get past them and pull out a victory, it would be the first time Everton had made it to the FA Cup Final since 1995, fourteen years before.

And how sweet would it be to beat the team that had made me feel so disposable?

The game was held at Wembley Stadium in London. It was the highest-attended FA Cup Semifinal in history— more than 88,000 fans. Half the stadium was given over to Manchester United fans, half to Everton fans.

One side red. The other side blue.

I'm sure that Manchester United and all those supporters in red thought they knew exactly what was going to happen in that game. They were sure they were going to win. After all, they were the big-budget team, the one that could afford to buy the world's most expensive players.

I was determined to prove them wrong.

From the start, shots were scarce, but we were scrappy. We kept Manchester United's chances to a minimum.

And when they did get a chance to score, I stopped the ball.

The game was scoreless by the half. Then again at the end of regulation time.

Extra time came and went, and still nobody scored. That meant we were heading for a penalty kick shootout. My favorite kind of showdown.

It would be me versus Manchester United.

I flashed back to 2005, when I'd been benched during the FA Cup Final. Ferguson had told me to warm up before the shoot-out . . . then never put me in the game.

Well, I was in the game now! This time, though, I was an Everton man. I was more confident than I'd been when I was at Man U. I had a stronger sense of self. And I'd spent the last few years playing—starting and playing—almost every single game. I'd developed skills I never could have while sitting on the bench.

I wanted to prove it.

The shoot-out would take place on Manchester

United's side. All around me, the stands were filled with red jerseys.

We were to kick first.

Everton's Tim Cahill took the first penalty. Ben Foster was the Manchester United keeper that day.

For Cahill's kick, Ben didn't need to do a thing. The ball sailed right over the bar.

Cahill dropped to his knees and placed his face into his hands. He was devastated. All around him, the Manchester United fans erupted gleefully. In that moment, I think they truly thought they were going to win this game.

My turn. I stopped a weak effort from Dimitar Berbatov. Still 0–0.

Our Leighton Baines drilled the ball into the net, and the blue side went wild. 1–0.

Then I faced Rio Ferdinand, my old teammate. Somehow I knew Rio was going right—I sensed it. I dove right, and reached long. Rio's kick was a hard drive, not easy to stop.

But stop it I did.

Phil Neville didn't flinch as he drove one in for Everton's side. He sent the ball to the lower left corner. Ben guessed which way the shot would go, and he guessed wrong; he dove in the other direction.

Boom. Now it was 2–0. We needed two more.

Manchester United's Nemanja Vidic added an unusual stutter step to his run-up. It threw me. I dove to my left, and Nemanja hit a strong shot to the other corner.

2–1.

Our James Vaughan sent a great strike to the upper right corner. Ben guessed correctly, but it was an amazing shot. Ben had no chance.

3–1.

Manchester United's Anderson kicked one way. I dove the other.

3–2.

And then our center back Phil Jagielka stepped up.

Ben took his place in goal.

I watched from the side. If Jags could score, we'd win this game. I made the sign of the cross. I watched and waited.

Jags had a fast run-up to the ball. He sent a hard shot to the lower right corner.

Jags nailed it!

And that meant we'd done it. We'd beaten Manchester United. On penalty kicks—the ultimate goalkeeper's triumph.

Five years ago, I'd helped Manchester United win the Community Shield on a penalty kick shoot-out. On that day, I'd been on the top of the world. Then I'd fallen from my perch.

And now, I'd helped my new team. It felt every bit as good as that Community Shield win had. Better.

As the blue side of Wembley went wild, I sprinted toward my teammates. I made it about fifteen yards from the goal area before I was wrestled to the ground by all those "Blue Boys"—my teammates, my friends. It was the best kind of mayhem. All of us were thrilled beyond measure.

We were going to the FA Cup Final.

Later, I'd learn that my old coach, Mulch, had been driving home from his son's soccer practice during the game. He'd gotten his wife on speakerphone during the drive, so she could give him the play-by-play. When it went to penalty kicks, he gripped the wheel as she described the action.

"Tim stopped that one. . . ."

"Shoot, that one got through. . . ."

When Jags kicked his winning shot into the net, Mulch and his son celebrated wildly inside the car. Mulch honked the horn, rolled down the window, and pumped his fist in celebration. He cheered and shouted.

The other drivers on the road gave him strange glances. Who was this oddball, and what exactly was he celebrating on the highway on a random Sunday in April?

Why was that weird redheaded guy so darned happy?

He was happy for me, of course. Mulch was still rooting for me after all these years.

Back in Wembley, I ran over to the fans in blue and held up my arms. A fan tossed an Everton scarf onto the field. I don't know who threw it. I will never know anything about that person's life—where they worked, or what their family was like, or what challenges they faced as they walked through this world.

But I knew this: they'd sent that scarf flying down to the field out of gratitude. I picked it up and raised it high over my head.

No, I wanted to say. *I'm the one who is grateful to you. I am grateful to all of you for being the greatest fans on earth.*

Later, in the locker room, I sat down next to Tony Hibbert. I was both elated and drained. I tossed my towel over my head to wipe the sweat from my face. And then something happened to me.

I was overcome by emotion.

Instead of removing the towel, I left it there. I sat for just a moment in the dark, surrounded by all the cheers and hollers of my teammates celebrating.

And before I understood what was happening, I clutched the towel to my face and began sobbing. I cried

Poppa, my mother, and Momma, at home in Hungary, before they had to escape under cover of night.

With big brother Chris and my mom, looking sharp in our '80s attire.

As a kid I hated sitting still.... I suspect I could barely sit still for this photo!

Chris was my fierce protector when I was young.

Photos are courtesy of the author unless otherwise noted.

As a child, I always stood head and shoulders above the other soccer players.

Being named one of the captains for the '96 high school soccer season by my legendary coach, Stan Williston.

To my mom's great relief, I managed to stay in school long enough to take this high school graduation photo!

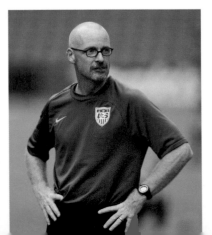

Tim Mulqueen: the man who made me the keeper I am today. He's been a coach and a mentor and is now a dear friend.

(Brad Smith/isiphotos.com)

The dream started at the MetroStars! Here I am, 21 years old...with still so much to learn. *(Courtesy of Major League Soccer)*

Meeting Sir Alex Ferguson for the first time...naively wearing Manchester City colors. *(John Peters/Manchester United/Getty Images)*

I couldn't have dreamed up a better start to my Manchester United career. We beat Arsenal in a shootout to win the 2003 Community Shield and I made the decisive save. Here I am with the guys accepting the silverware *(from left to right)*: Ryan Giggs, Rio Ferdinand, Eric Djemba-Djemba, Nicky Butt, Ruud van Nistelrooy, Paul Scholes, and Darren Fletcher. *(John Peters/Manchester United/Getty Images)*

The perfect wedding was planned in only three days.

Nana in her Sunday best at my wedding in Central Park.

Everyone adored sweet baby Jacob... everyone but Clayton!

Ali was a live wire right from the start.

Two things Ali likes most: the ocean and her big brother, Jacob.

My Everton mates celebrating with me after we beat Manchester United on PKs. *(Javier Garcia/ BPI/isiphotos.com)*

Nothing was more rewarding than a handshake from my goalkeeping coach, Chris Woods, after a big win. *(Chris Brunskill/BPI/ isiphotos.com)*

I'd run into a burning building for this man, David Moyes. *(Jamie McDonald/Getty Images)*

My day job on a Saturday morning. *(Matt West/isiphotos.com)*

"Before" shot: throwing the ball to Landon near the end of the 2010 World Cup game against Algeria. *(Perry McIntyre/isiphotos. com)*

"After" shot: celebrating Landon's game-winning goal against Algeria. *(Phil Cole/Getty Images)*

Me and my pal Carlos after the last qualification game vs. Costa Rica, 2009. Thanks to the fan who threw me this hat! *(John Todd/isiphotos.com)*

In our 2014 World Cup game against Portugal, I changed direction mid-dive to scoop Eder's point-blank shot over the crossbar. It's one of my all-time-favorite saves. *(Elsa/Getty Images)*

One of my 15 saves against Belgium. *(Yves Herman/Reuters/Corbis)*

Brotherhood transcends even the toughest moments on the field: with Romelu Lukaku after the 2014 World Cup game against Belgium. *(Kieran McManus/isiphotos.com)*

Tess and Paige Kowalski, two of the many incredible kids I've met with Tourette Syndrome. *(Courtesy of the Kowalski family)*

Mom, Dad, and the kids sharing my proudest moment with me: my 100th cap for the U.S. national team.

I am calmest, most at peace, when my children are close.

like a small child. I cried like I hadn't since my days in Northwood Estates—loud, choking sobs. I suddenly understood how much Man U had gotten under my skin, how much that experience had stayed with me.

Now, for the first time, I could let them go.

I didn't care that my teammates could see my shoulders shake. Didn't care that my crying could be heard over the sounds of their laughter.

I didn't care what anyone thought. I was just so glad that I'd done this.

Phil Jagielka noticed. "Hey, Tim? You all right?"

Then Tony Hibbert's voice. "Yeah. He's all right." I felt his hand on my back. "He just needs a moment."

Hibbo understood. He understood without my telling him. He realized, just like Mulch did back in the States, exactly what this game meant for me.

It was just a semifinal, mind you. We hadn't won the FA Cup Final. In fact, we wouldn't. We'd lose to Chelsea 2–1, despite taking a 1–0 lead just twenty-five seconds into the game. And that loss would hurt, in the way that losses always do.

But as I sat in the Wembley locker room with that towel pressed against my face, I wasn't thinking about the game ahead.

Right now, all I heard in my head was a single line on

endless repeat. I'd text that line to Mulch after leaving the locker room—just four words, but they said everything.

I slayed the dragon.

Faith Rice, the woman who had organized all those Tourette Syndrome events for the MetroStars, called me soon after that.

"Listen, Tim," she said. "I've got a great idea. I need your help."

Faith had been working away back in New Jersey. The organization she'd started, now called the New Jersey Center for Tourette Syndrome, NJCTS, was doing everything it could to provide support and education for families with TS.

"But we need to do more," she said. She explained that one of the great cruelties of TS is that the symptoms tend to peak in adolescence, precisely when kids are dealing with so many other big changes.

"I want to create a leadership academy for teens," she said. The academy, as she envisioned it, would teach them the skills they'd need to navigate adult life with TS. It would teach them exactly what TS was, and how it worked. That way, teens could find the words to explain their conditions to others. It would help them cope with the added social stress of being a kid with TS.

"Most of all," she added, "the leadership academy will give them the tools to find their own strengths."

It was a good idea. To be honest, I would have loved to have had something like that when I was a kid. I wished that I had known how to ask for help, how to talk about this condition I had instead of hiding it until I could get away from the classroom.

Who knows how something like that would have changed those years for me.

Maybe if I'd had that kind of support, I could have slayed a different dragon even sooner. Maybe I could have conquered, earlier, some of my own shame about my TS.

"Faith," I said, "I love the idea. Let me know what I can do to help."

"For now, you just keep playing soccer," she said. "I'll keep working on this end. I'll let you know when I need you."

PART THREE

CHAPTER 16
AMERICA, SOCCER NATION?

THE UNITED STATES BEGAN ACCOMPLISHING SOME AMAZING things in soccer.

In 2007, we had gone to the Gold Cup, the continental championship.

That tournament had been the start of a new era. Bob Bradley, my old MetroStars coach, had become the coach for the national team. Bob named my old friend Carlos the team's new captain. What a great captain he would make: he still had the same, quiet, steady presence he'd had when we were on the Youth National Team together.

In that tournament, I'd been moved into the starting

goalkeeper slot, above Kasey Keller.

We had a good team. These were guts-and-glory guys, not an overblown ego in the bunch. Landon was there, and by now he had become as much of a super-star as any American had ever been. He was three years younger than I was. Last year, he had become the US all-time assist leader, with twenty-three assists. By the end of this year, he'd score his thirty-fifth international goal and reach a hundred caps (games) for the US team. Bob Bradley's son, Michael, had also joined the team.

I liked these teammates every bit as much as I liked my Everton mates, and I loved the melting-pot feel of our team. We were black and white and every shade in between—the sons of truckers and teachers and oil men and military parents. And none of the differences mattered one bit.

During the group stage of the tournament, we achieved the best first-round record in our group. We beat all the teams we played: Ecuador, Trinidad and Tobago, and El Salvador. We scored seven goals, and we conceded none. We moved up to the quarterfinals, and we narrowly beat Panama. In the semifinals, we knocked out Canada.

That meant we'd be going to the finals, where we'd meet Mexico.

Our archrivals.

It was a tough game. Mexico dominated for a long time, and just before the half, Mexico hammered in a goal from close range. I dove for it and missed. When I landed on the ground, I landed hard. The Mexican fans celebrated wildly. I couldn't tell if my head was vibrating from the pandemonium in the stands, or from the fall I'd just had.

But in the second half, we earned a penalty kick. Landon stepped up and coolly slotted the ball home. 1–1.

With twenty minutes left on the clock, Landon took a corner kick. It was cleared by the Mexican defense, but only to the edge of the box. There, a US player, Benny Feilhaber, was lurking, all alone.

I saw Benny lift his leg. From my vantage point, it was clear he shouldn't take the shot. He was too far out. The penalty area was packed with Mexican players. *Don't do it,* I thought.

A couple of our guys even screamed it. "No!"

Benny paid them no mind. One touch, and he sent the ball into the goal. The ball flew past a mass of Mexican defenders. It went past their stunned keeper. Later, the *New York Times* would call it "perhaps the greatest, the best, the most technically impressive goal scored in the long, long history of soccer in the United States."

About a second and a half earlier, nobody wanted

Benny to take the shot. Now, everyone ran toward him in celebration.

Although Mexico amped up the pressure after that, they couldn't score. We won.

And just like that, we were the best team in North America.

We were showered with confetti as our national anthem played. When Carlos lifted the Gold Cup—it was enormous, the size of a second grader—we were all jumping up and down like little kids on a trampoline.

There were a handful of soccer diehards who paid attention to that win. But for the most part, nobody in America had any idea. After the game, Carlos and some of the other guys had taken the huge Gold Cup trophy out to dinner. It got some attention. People asked, "What is that thing? Who are you guys?" But nobody recognized the team. Some strangers were even surprised that the US had a soccer team, let alone one that had just shifted the balance of power in the Americas.

A decade after the MLS had started, America was still not a soccer nation.

That Gold Cup win earned us entry to the Confederations Cup in 2009, a tournament of eight champions. There were some outstanding teams in that tournament—best in the world teams—including Brazil, Spain, and Italy.

And though our first couple of games were disasters, we somehow—through some miracle of the scoreboard that I barely understand today—managed to advance.

In the semifinals, we met Spain.

At that point, Spain was the world's top-ranked team. Spain had beaten all of Europe in the UEFA Cup tournament. They'd been unbeaten in their last thirty-five games . . . and their most recent seventeen had been victories. They hadn't conceded a single goal in the tournament so far . . . whereas we'd conceded six.

Pretty intimidating for the USA!

We surprised ourselves by taking the lead in that game, with a powerful shot by Jozy Altidore from twenty-five yards. Spain fought back hard. They attacked relentlessly. They dominated the field. But I'll tell you: our defense was on lockdown that day. Every time Spain tried to move the ball forward, a US player was clearing it away.

I was so proud of our defense, so proud of this team of ours. We weren't just holding our own against the best team in the world . . . we were actually up by a goal.

Late in the game, we scored a second time, off a deflection.

We were up by two goals now. Against Spain. It was so surreal, I had to remind myself it was actually happening.

The clock ticked down fast, and the game had ended 2–0.

It barely made sense. We had beaten the best team in the world!

When the whistle blew, I dropped to my knees. I looked toward the heavens and I spoke out loud.

"I don't know why," I said. I kissed my goalkeeper's gloves. "And I don't know why me. But thank you."

We played Brazil in the finals of the Confederations Cup tournament, and we lost 3–2.

But the game was a victory in a way that had nothing to do with the scoreboard. Something had changed.

For the first time, people were watching.

We learned later that the final was the most-watched non–World Cup game in our team's history.

Worldwide, fifty-eight million viewers had tuned in. Nearly four million of those were in the US.

When I started playing this sport professionally, nobody cared about it. Soccer was a kids' game. It wasn't a sport that men took seriously.

You had to leave the country to play in any serious way.

But look: now we'd beaten the number-one team in the world. We'd taken second place in one of the biggest worldwide tournaments. We were playing well . . .

and for the first time in my professional life, millions of Americans were paying attention.

Could it be that soccer was finally making gains in the last non-soccer nation on earth?

CHAPTER 17
2010: "LOOK AT ME NOW, POPPA"

WELL, THIS IS SURREAL.

I was standing in the West Wing of the White House.

Everything around me was exactly like I'd seen it a hundred times before. I'd seen this setting in movies. I'd seen it on television. I'd seen it in textbooks, and in news reports. There were the battle flags, the heavily framed portraits of past presidents, the round eagle carpet in the middle of the Oval Office.

But the angles had gone all funny; somehow I was in the middle of the picture, as if I'd unzipped a television screen and walked right onto the set.

It was 2010. Tomorrow we'd be heading to South

Africa. Our destination was the 2010 World Cup. First, though, we had come to DC, as honored guests of the White House.

Me. Timmy Howard, the kid who hadn't been able to sit still in his classroom. A guest of the president of the United States.

Our team wasn't getting just any old tour, either. Vice President Joe Biden had given us a full thirty minutes. He'd spoken to each of us personally, asking us questions about where we were from, what teams we played for when we weren't playing for the USA.

Then former president Bill Clinton had come in to shake our hands. Clinton would even be attending the World Cup in South Africa.

And now we were shaking hands with President Obama himself. Obama was laughing and relaxed, like we were old friends.

"This is incredible," Carlos whispered to me.

"You bet it is," I whispered back.

A crisply dressed woman clapped her hands at us. "We're going to take a photograph now," she said. "Please follow us outside to the steps."

We opened the doors and stepped out into the DC summer. It was sweltering out there—ninety-three degrees and humid. Our team was dressed alike, in khakis and precisely matched brown leather shoes, dress shirts, and heavy warm-up jackets emblazoned with the US Soccer logo.

As Clinton and Obama and Biden mingled with the team, we all wiped sweat off our brows, trying not to look like we were melting in the heat.

Standing there, I kept thinking about my poppa, my mother's dad.

Poppa had passed away last September. Because I was in England, I hadn't been able to go to the funeral.

I wished like crazy he were still around. I wished I could share this moment with him.

What would he have thought, if someone had told him on the night he was fleeing Hungary for his life, that someday his grandson would stand in the White House?

You will escape, they might have said. *And you will succeed in your new country. And one day your grandson, the child of the little girl whom you're trying so desperately to hush, will stand at the White House flanked by the most important leaders in the world.*

My thoughts were broken by President Obama.

"I just wanted to say how incredibly proud we are of the team," he said. "We are incredibly proud of what you've done already, and we are going to be proud of what you do when you get to South Africa."

It's hard to describe what it felt like to be standing there on the brink of my first World Cup start. I'd been eleven years old back in 1990, when the US qualified for the World Cup for the first time in forty years. I'd watched us play in that tournament on a grainy television in my mother's living room, with no earthly idea what might lie ahead. Since then, I'd marched steadily toward this moment. I'd been in the stands in '94, with Mulch pointing down to the field, saying, "That should be you." By '98, I'd been playing side by side on the MetroStars with Tony Meola, the US World Cup goalkeeper. By 2002, I was friends with a bunch of guys on the team, and I'd earned a spot as the number-four keeper—not enough to attend the tournament, but getting closer. Then in 2006, I'd sat on the bench watching Kasey.

Now it was my turn.

The camera shutters clicked as sweat trickled down my neck. Bill Clinton was so close to me that I could have reached over and patted him on the back.

In the photograph that was published later that day, I'm beaming like a little kid.

We trained for the 2010 World Cup in Princeton, New Jersey. While I was there, I was able to spend time with my brother before leaving for South Africa.

I missed Chris. Once upon a time, he'd been my constant companion. He'd been my protector and my best friend. I had followed him, day and night, through Northwood Estates—the same way that my Ali, now three, followed Jacob, now five.

Back then, I'd assumed it would always be that way: that Chris would be by my side forever.

These days, though, between my training and games, I almost never saw my brother. I was too busy shuffling back and forth between my Everton games and my US National Team games.

I loved him as much as I ever did. I'd cemented his role in our family's life by making him Jacob's godfather. It was a role we both took seriously.

But we lived thousands of miles away from each other. I saw Carlos and Landon and Bob Bradley far more than I saw Chris. Heck, I saw the Liverpool and Mexico team players more than I saw Chris . . . and I couldn't stand those guys.

So that month in Jersey had been great. It had given us a chance to spend some quality time together—just two brothers, laughing about a shared past.

Before I left for South Africa, he'd written me a note, along with a quote from Heracleitus, an ancient Greek philosopher. The quote said:

A WARRIOR
Out of every one hundred men, ten shouldn't even
be there,
Eighty are just targets,
Nine are the real fighters,
and we are lucky to have them,
for they make the battle.

Ah, but the one,
One is a warrior,
And he will bring the others back.
—Heracleitus

Then he'd written:

Good luck in WC 2010!!
You will bring them back.

I read that quote again and again.
Good luck in WC 2010!! You will bring them back.
And I wanted to.

We flew through night and day to get to South Africa.
The flight was seventeen hours in all. Then we climbed
aboard a bus and rode for many hours more. By the
time the bus rolled to a stop at the lodge where we'd

be spending the next month—our home base for training and the World Cup tournament—I had no idea how long we'd been traveling, or even what time zone we were in. All I knew was that it was dark outside, and I was wiped out.

As the bus doors opened, we heard voices rising up into the night. A traditional South African choir greeted us. They sang in a language I didn't understand, but their tone said, *Welcome. Welcome to our home at the far southern tip of this continent. Welcome to everything that is about to happen. Welcome to the World Cup, the biggest soccer stage there is.*

In the morning, when I woke after a long sleep, I stepped out onto the balcony of my room to look around.

Outside, across a lake, my teammate Clint Dempsey sat perfectly still, fishing rod in his hand. He was wearing a camouflage hat. Clint had grown up in a small town in Texas. Now he might be halfway around the world, but he was doing the thing he loved best: fishing like the country boy he was.

We were isolated at that lodge—far from the rest of the world, with lots of time on our hands. Our sole jobs were to train until we had nothing left, then rest so we could do it again the next day. We trained together and ate together and relaxed together.

You'd think that spending that much time with the

same group of guys—all of us in one isolated location that's nearly ten thousand miles from home—might present some challenges.

You'd think, for example, we might start getting on one another's nerves.

But that was the thing about this team. We never got on one another's nerves.

On the bus rides to and from the gym, guys threw gum wrappers at one another, mocked one another about their haircuts. We horsed around and teased each other endlessly.

Jay DeMerit and Stuart Holden often belted out Justin Bieber songs at the top of their lungs, and the rest of the guys groaned.

Then in the afternoons we'd all hang out together. Music wafted across the air, and we knew that someone was just rocking out in his room. Once in a while, some jokester might throw water on another player while they were out on their balcony reading. We were like a bunch of playful puppies. We'd tumble all over one another, roughhouse together. Then we'd retreat to our separate rooms, sleep, and wake up ready to start all over again.

We had the kind of togetherness that is rare in this world. It's like we were more than just guys who played on a team together. We were brothers.

Maybe there's something about soccer being a team

sport. Or maybe it's the fact that we weren't just soccer players, we were American soccer players. That means we were mostly unknown to our nation, fighting for respect both at home and abroad.

Maybe it was just something about this group of guys in particular.

At any rate, it's hard to imagine that any other collection of pro athletes would ever be so easy to be around for so long.

So relaxed, so humble. So darned much fun.

Even in our downtime, though, our coach, Bob Bradley, never quit. He never, ever stopped thinking about the game.

He walked around the lodge with a portable DVD player. It didn't matter where we were—on the field, on the bus, in our hotel rooms, eating dinner. When we saw Bob hauling that thing around, we knew he had something to show us—clips of opposing team plays, or maybe of ourselves playing, something he thought we could do better.

"Uh-oh," Carlos might say when he saw Bob coming. "Better hide in the bushes, Bob's got his DVD player out again."

"Shh. Don't make eye contact," I'd joke in response.

But Bob would just walk up, grab one of us, and press play.

"You see where you are here," he would say. He'd point to a clip from a recent game. "Next time, I want you to get five yards over so their winger can't make that pass."

Whoever he was talking to always nodded. The truth is, Bob was always right.

In the tournament, we would play England, then upstart Slovenia, then Algeria.

When the England match was just a few days away, I sat on the bus on the way to training, jiggling my leg nervously. Stuart and Jay were two rows ahead of me.

Naturally, those clowns were singing Bieber again.

"Baby, baby, baby, oh . . ."

Landon threw half a granola bar at them. The bar landed on the seat, Jay leaned over, picked it up, and popped it in his mouth, still singing. Crumbs fell out of his mouth, but he kept belting out that song.

"Like, baby, baby, baby, no . . ."

But I already felt myself drifting into my pregame mode. If my churning stomach didn't tell me that I was gearing up for the big game, my constant tics sure did.

I kept thinking about that quote from my brother.

You will bring them back.

I wanted to be the warrior. Oh, man, I wanted that so badly.

* * *

By the time we were on the way to our first game, against England, the mood on the bus had shifted completely.

Nobody sang. Nobody talked.

We listened to music on our headphones, each lost in his own world of mental preparation. I knew that all my teammates—Carlos, Landon, everyone—felt the same pressure I did.

Something big was in our grasp—something huge. I could feel it. We wanted to reach out and grab it.

Even in the locker room suiting up, we were almost completely silent. We looked at white tactics boards, listened to final instructions from Bob.

Then Carlos said, "Let's do this for each other."

I wanted to get as far in this tournament as we possibly could. That desire came from the deepest part of me—my DNA, my soul.

We walked out to the field. I took my place in goal in my first-ever World Cup match.

That game against England proved that no one should dismiss the American team. Ever. England was the clear favorite, their roster packed with players from the Premier League. They took control of the game almost immediately. After a few minutes on the clock, England's Emile Heskey sent a reverse pass to Steven Gerrard.

Gerrard slotted it past me with ease.

Just four minutes in, we were down by one.

Then, twenty-nine minutes in, I was injured. Badly.

I made a diving save. I parried away the ball at the same moment Heskey came sliding toward it. His foot was extended, and his studs were up. He was positioned to slam a ball into the net, not to meet flesh and bone.

Even in that split second as he came toward me, I thought, *This is bad.*

Heskey's foot crashed into my rib cage. Hard. It sent me flying backward. I understood then why people talk about blinding pain. My chest hurt so bad I could barely see.

As our Steve Cherundolo cleared the ball, I just lay there on the ground, my hand on my chest.

When I didn't get up, doctors ran to the field.

"Is something broken?" I asked. It was all I could do to speak. "I don't know what's going on, is something broken?"

"You want to come off, Tim?"

Oh God. No. No, I didn't.

I managed to stand. "Let me see how I do."

It hurt like crazy, but I stayed in the game. I'd come so far. I'd waited so long. How could I possibly stop now, just a half hour in?

In the fortieth minute Clint Dempsey sent a shot

rolling toward England's goal. It looked like their keeper, Robert Green, was scooping it up.

But wait, hold on—he wasn't.

The ball went beneath Green. It rolled right through his legs.

We watched it crawl across the line in a kind of disbelief. That was truly a goalkeeper's worst nightmare . . . and on the biggest stage possible.

And just like that, we were even.

I felt terrible for Green. I remembered how it felt to fumble the ball in the final moments of that Champions League match against FC Porto, back when I played for Man U. I knew how awful he must feel. That's the tough thing about being a goalkeeper: the ball might go past ten other guys by the time it gets to you . . . but it's your errors that are on glaring display for the world to see.

The second half of the match was thrilling. England had plenty of chances, but we held the line. The game ended in a 1–1 draw.

President Obama called the team to congratulate us on our tie, our gutsy performance. In the middle of the phone call, he said, "And Tim . . . how are those ribs of yours doing?"

I was so taken aback, I didn't know what to say.

My response was simple—"I'm okay, thanks, Mr. President." But I was so caught off guard, so afraid of messing up and saying the wrong thing, that my voice cracked. I sounded like a little old lady instead of a professional athlete.

To this day, some of my teammates still make fun of me for that one.

Slovenia was another come-from-behind draw.

It was one of those hard-fought, back-and-forth dramas that proves what an exciting game soccer can be.

Both sides had plenty of chances in the first forty-five minutes. But by the half, Slovenia had converted two of them. We, on the other hand, had converted zero. The score was 2–0.

That momentum shifted early in the second half. Landon made a surging run on goal from the right flank. Slovenian defenders slid into his path. If he was going to shoot, he'd have to do it from an impossibly tight angle.

He tried. The ball flew right into the upper corner of the net. Goal!

It was as skillful a shot as you'll ever see from that position.

I could just feel the game turn in that moment. Cries of "USA! USA!" rang out. We were back in it!

In the eighty-second minute, Landon sent the ball toward Jozy Altidore. Jozy headed it toward Michael Bradley. Michael charged forward and drilled the ball right into the roof of the goal.

2–2.

Then, with the clock nearing the eighty-fifth minute, Landon earned a free kick.

He floated it toward the goal. There was our Maurice Edu, who redirected it into the net. It was a thrilling finish . . . or it would have been.

It should have been.

But the referee blew his whistle. The goal wouldn't be allowed. There had apparently been some sort of foul. But what foul? Edu wasn't offsides. Nobody saw any foul. Our players surrounded the ref, asking him to explain why he'd made that call.

"Just tell us what the call is."

"Where was the foul?"

We begged and pleaded, but the referee didn't answer. He didn't answer then, and later FIFA would restrict him from ever saying why he blew the whistle. His call was the call, and that was that.

Since that moment, Edu's goal has been replayed tens of thousands of times. It's been slowed down frame by frame. Every split second has been analyzed and dissected. To this day, no one can tell me why it didn't count.

Here's what I see when I look at freeze-frames of the action: I see a Slovenian defender holding his arm out, forcefully blocking Edu's run toward the ball. I see another Slovenian defender bear-hugging Michael from behind—pinning Michael's arms. I see Carlos being smothered by one of the Slovenians; Jozy being gripped from the side. Jay's being held by a Slovenian, too.

In fact, in all of this grabbing and shoving, I see just a single American—Clint—holding on to any Slovenian player at all. And that player's not even near the ball.

There had been no foul. We'd just been hosed, that's all.

The game ended in a 2–2 draw.

Which meant if we were going to advance to the knockout round, we had to beat Algeria.

I will never forget our arrival at the Loftus Versfeld, the Pretoria stadium where we'd play our do-or-die match against Algeria.

We knew former president Clinton would be at that game. So we'd expected longer security waits. We'd expected traffic and buzzing helicopters overhead.

But we hadn't anticipated the reception that was waiting for us.

Long before we arrived at Loftus, American fans were on the road. There were thousands of them. They were waving and cheering at our bus.

When Loftus came into view, the team bus rolled to a stop. We had entered a sea of fans. They were all wearing red, white, and blue. These fans were stretched out in all directions. Some had wrapped themselves in American flags. Others rocked Mohawks dyed in our national colors. There were fans with painted faces and American flag T-shirts.

These fans held up scarves like you might see at a Premier League match, except these ones said "Land of the Free."

The fans waved to us. They called out "Good luck." They rapped on our bus windows, screaming, "USA!"

By this point, I was accustomed to playing in international games where nobody cared about our team. I mean, every time we played Mexico—even on our own home turf—nearly every fan in the stadium wore a green shirt!

We gaped at them through the windows. We were so far from home—halfway around the world—and yet all these fans made us feel like we were home.

"Holy cow," murmured Carlos as he stared out at all that red, white, and blue. "This is awesome."

A bunch of the guys gave thumbs-up signs to the crowd. Jay and Stuart pounded the window and cheered right back at those fans.

* * *

The Algeria game was scoreless for a full ninety minutes. Their keeper made some good saves. We hit the post a few times. We had a goal called back because of offsides. But the board remained stubbornly 0–0.

We were holding our own, but a draw wouldn't be good enough; to advance, we had to win.

Toward the end of the game, things got desperate. Tactics went out the window. Defensive principles? Gone.

The ball pinged back and forth across the field. Algeria would possess the ball, then attack. We'd steal it back, then attack.

I watched on full alert, trying to keep my defenders in some kind of organized shape. But this was our last gasp. We were minutes from being knocked out of the tournament, and we were running on empty. We had to give the game everything we had.

Then, in the ninety-first minute, Algeria's Rafik Saïfi headed the ball toward our goal from the left.

The ball bounced, and I caught it.

Seconds from the end, and the ball was in my hands, at the wrong end of the field.

I had to move fast —really, really fast. Somehow, I had to get the ball to a place where someone could score.

There was no time to think; I had to operate only on instinct.

And my instincts had been formed on those fields

in New Jersey. They had been formed by Mulch drilling certain lessons into me again and again.

When the ball comes in from the left, look to the right, Mulch always said.

I didn't even have to look. I knew—I just knew—that Landon was tearing down the right-hand side.

A split second after I got the ball—almost no time had passed whatsoever—I threw it long. I threw it to Landon.

It landed at his feet, just like Mulch always insisted it should.

Landon took the ball and blazed forward.

Jozy was in the penalty box; Landon got the ball to him.

Jozy crossed it to Clint. Clint got a touch. Their keeper charged out of the goal.

The ball bounced off the keeper, away from the goal. Just for a moment, it looked to most of the world like it was just another failed attempt.

It looked to most of the world like we'd be going home.

But I had my eye on Landon. He was still running. I watched as he moved toward the ball as it moved away from the Algerian net. I'm not sure the defender even knew he was there. That's the thing about Landon. He doesn't broadcast his presence like some of the flashier players. He just glides in, completely cool. Quiet.

Stealthy.

There were ninety-two minutes on the clock. The ball had traveled from goal line to goal line in a few historic seconds.

Landon buried the ball in the back of the Algerian net.

He changed the scoreboard. It was too late for Algeria to come back now.

We'd won.

Landon raced toward the corner flag. He stretched out his arms and dove, bodysurfing along the grass.

Benny Feilhaber slid behind him in celebration. Then everyone got in on it. All the guys on the field. All the guys on the bench. The coaches. The staff. Everyone. They ran toward Landon and threw themselves on top of him, one after another.

Jozy flew onto the pileup like he was Superman. Jay Demerit finished it off with a rolling somersault over the whole gang.

I watched the jubilation from the far end of the field.

I kneeled down and touched the grass, five precise touches.

I stood. I kissed my goalkeeper's gloves and raised my arms toward the sky. And just like I'd done after the Spain game, I thanked God for what had just happened.

We had advanced beyond the group stage. We were going to the knockout round.

I got to be a part of it.

"Thank you," I said, looking up. "Thank you."

In the locker room, we learned that former president Clinton was waiting in the hallway. He wanted to congratulate us.

Carlos turned to me. "I want to invite him in," he said.

Carlos wasn't wearing a shirt. He was dripping with sweat.

"To the locker room?" I asked.

Carlos nodded. "Why not?"

When I thought about it, I couldn't think of a reason. "Do it," I said. "That'd be sweet."

So Carlos, shirtless and sweaty, approached the former president of the United States and said, "Sir? We'd be honored if you'd join us in the locker room for our celebration."

That's exactly what President Clinton did. He rolled up his sleeves and hung out with us for a long time. I don't know what he talked to other guys about, but I remember talking to him about Arkansas, his home state. Laura and I sometimes vacationed there with the kids. Clinton and I also talked about books, and my children, and Landon, and the incredible game we'd just played.

And again, my thoughts returned to my poppa.

Look at me now, Poppa. I'm not just meeting a former president, I'm hanging out with him.

You had to flee Hungary for your life.

Mom had to scrimp and save every day of her life.

I got this thing called TS, which made life really hard sometimes. But America is the greatest country in the world, because here I am, and it feels amazing.

I hope you're enjoying watching this up there.

We played Ghana in the knockout round. We felt strong going in.

We genuinely believed we could handle them. And then we lost.

They scored early. We equalized on a late penalty. It went to extra time, and they scored again.

I took a lot of criticism for that goal from both sportscasters and fans. What I can say for sure is I gave my heart and soul to the game. I wanted to win more than I wanted anything. But once in a while, it happens.

Sometimes the game is beautiful, and sometimes it's cruel.

That was a cruel, cruel day.

In the locker room, everyone was quiet. Everyone's eyes were cast downward, staring at the floor—such a stark contrast to the mood after the Algeria game.

President Clinton walked in again. He shook every one of our hands. And then he addressed us as a group.

"Guys," he said, "it's never fun getting your butt kicked."

I glanced over at Carlos. His eyes were red.

"It's happened to me again and again," Clinton continued. "This won't be the last time it happens to you. But you're going to keep picking yourselves up."

He spoke the hardest truth—we had gotten our butts kicked. We would get our butts kicked again. It would feel just as terrible the next time as it did right now.

But he was right about something else: somehow we had to bounce back. We had to move forward.

We thanked him, and he left quietly.

We just showered off. Then we got out of there as soon as we could.

CHAPTER 18
THE KIND OF FATHER I WANT TO BE

AFTER I CAME HOME FROM THE 2010 WORLD CUP, LAURA AND I split up. I loved her, and I know she loved me. But my constant travel and my crazy every-seven-days game schedule had sucked all the energy out of our marriage.

Playing soccer professionally is hard on a family. You're constantly separated. Your mind's always on the game. The moment you play one game, the next game is just a few days away.

Laura and I were worn down after all these years.

Laura decided she would stay in Memphis, with her family. Who could blame her? If she wasn't going to be married to me, there was no reason for her to be in England anymore.

But it meant the kids were going to live in Memphis. Without me.

Jacob and Ali were my heartbeat. I couldn't imagine living apart from them. I couldn't imagine not having Ali crawl into bed and lay her tiny head on my chest in the morning, or not hearing the sound of Jacob's laughter echoing through the house.

Those kids were my everything, and now we would be living on different continents.

Three days after we filed the divorce papers, Everton played its first League match of the season, against the Blackburn Rovers.

I'll never forget that game.

In the fourteenth minute, Blackburn headed the ball into my box. Three of us charged toward it at the same time: me, Everton's center back Sylvain Distin, and Blackburn forward Nikola Kalinić. There was nothing unusual about the way the ball was moving. There was nothing odd about how we went for it—I'd lived a thousand moments like this one already.

Sylvain saw me coming and got out of the way so I could grab the ball. Kalinić was still barreling toward me, as any good striker would.

But the ball was secure. Safe. I had it in my hands.

My plan was to roll it out to my teammate Leighton Baines, let him take it down the left side of the field.

But as I went to roll the ball, I dropped it. It fell right to Kalinić's feet.

The striker couldn't believe his luck. He slotted the ball into the wide-open net. It was a terrible, terrible mistake on my part.

That was the only goal of the game; we lost 1–0.

Opening day of the season, and I'd made a spectacular blunder. I felt like I had when I was a kid and I let another player score on me. Back then, my mom would move her chair closer to me and make me feel better.

But my mom was on the other side of the ocean now. All my family was.

As I walked off the field, my goalkeeping coach, Chris Woods, shook my hand and patted me on the back just as he always does. But I knew David Moyes would be furious.

He was. "I don't understand," he hissed. "What were you doing? What were you *thinking*?"

The next day, I barely got out of bed. I lay there, thinking, *I can't believe it. I can't believe I let my team down like that.*

I didn't feel any better the next day. But I couldn't miss practice, and besides: I needed to talk to Moyes. If anyone needed—and deserved—to know what was happening in my personal life, it would be him. So I dragged myself out of bed early on Monday and drove to the training ground.

From Everton's parking lot you can see into Moyes's glass-walled corner office. I saw Moyes already there, sitting upright at his desk.

I took a deep breath before entering the building. Upstairs, I knocked on his door. "David?" I asked. "Can I come in?"

Moyes looked up. "Sure, Tim, sit down."

So I did. But when I tried to speak, the words wouldn't come. I opened my mouth, closed it, stared at the floor. Right here, in front of me, was a man who'd put his absolute faith and trust in me, unconditionally, and I'd let him down. I'd let the fans down, too. My teammates.

Heck, I'd let myself down.

"Tim?" he asked gently. "What's going on?"

It was only when my eyes filled with tears that I managed to speak.

"I just need you to know where I'm at personally," I began. "Laura and I are getting a divorce. The kids are going to stay with her in Memphis."

The words coming out of my mouth sounded so cold. So cruel. Could they even be my words?

"Tim," he said. "Look, I had no idea. If I'd known, I never would have reacted the way I—"

I held my hands up. "Stop," I said. "You had every right to react that way. I'm a big boy, and I made a big mistake. I can handle it. I just thought . . . I just wanted you to know."

He nodded, and we sat there silently for a few long moments.

"If you need anything," Moyes finally said, "you just tell me."

"Okay, thanks."

"I mean it. Come around to my house anytime. Day or night. Nothing's off-limits, you hear me? We'll sit. We'll talk."

We stood up and shook hands. Then I headed down to the locker room to change, all the while thinking, *David Moyes, you might be steely. You might have a temper. But you are a diamond of a human being.*

Discreetly, David let Chris Woods and some of the senior players in on the news. One by one, they approached me. They told me how sorry they were. They invited me to dinner. They told me that whenever I felt like talking, they'd be around to listen.

After a while, everyone at Everton knew. Even cranky Jimmy Martin shook my hand. "I'm sorry about your personal trouble," he said. Then he handed me three sets of white socks. "You let me know if you need any more, okay?"

That season, Everton became my sanctuary. I lived alone in a big empty house that had once been filled with children's laughter. I didn't really want to be there all alone. So I'd go into training an hour or two early.

I'd train, and then I'd hang around hours after everyone else left. I'd eat lunch. I'd talk to the staff who worked in the kitchen. I'd hang out with Jimmy Martin and listen to him grumble. I got more physiotherapy than I needed. I just wanted to be surrounded by the people who felt as much like family as I had in England.

When I told my mom about the divorce, she mostly listened, the same way she always has.

She asked just a single question. "How are you going to be apart from the kids?" It was one of the only times in my life that I heard true anguish in her voice.

I'd already thought through all the possible ways I might be able stay close to the kids. I'd racked my brain, trying to figure out how we could live on the same continent. I could return to the States, try to get picked up by an MLS team. There was no MLS team in Memphis, though, and I'd still have trainings all week, games every weekend. I'd still see them only occasionally.

Besides, playing for the Premier League, I made enough money that I could retire comfortably in

Memphis permanently by the time I was forty—before the kids were in high school.

If I worked for an MLS team, I'd have to play far longer to be able to retire.

So I told my mom the only thing I knew for sure.

"Mom," I said, "it's on me to be the kind of father I want to be."

A few weeks after talking to David Moyes in his office, I missed my kids so much I didn't think I could stand it anymore.

Ali and Jacob lived 4,200 miles away. In Memphis, the school year had started. They had teachers and friends I'd never met.

There's no scheduled time off for Premier League teams. By tradition, we'll get the day after a game, usually Sunday, off, and one other day that week, typically Wednesday—but not two consecutive days off when I'd be able to travel.

But I missed my kids so much.

I asked David Moyes for permission to fly home after the upcoming Saturday match. My plan was this: Leave England on Sunday morning. Arrive in Memphis on Sunday evening. Spend all day Monday with Ali and Jacob. Drive them to school Tuesday, then head straight to the airport. Fly to England, arriving Wednesday morning.

The rest of the team would have that day off, but I'd go straight to the field and train as long and as hard as I could to make up for some of the time I'd missed.

It was an almost unheard-of arrangement, but Moyes fixed those serious eyes on me and nodded. "Absolutely," he said. "You go see your kids."

I did.

During that trip, I wrapped my arms around those beautiful children. I held Ali in my lap, pressed her wild tangles against my cheek as Clayton—that sweet old dog—tried to scramble up onto the sofa with us. I listened as Jacob told me about his new school, his new friends.

I heard my kids laugh, and I laughed with them.

And although the trip was brief, and I had to turn around and go back to England almost as soon as I'd arrived, I felt renewed.

That trip gave me the energy to keep moving forward. It kept me going.

In early November, Moyes approached me. I'd been feeling dark and jittery, easily frustrated on the field. "You need to see your kids again?" he asked.

"Yeah," I said. "I really do."

So he let me make the trip again.

And again. Every few weeks for the rest of that season and most of the next, I traveled on the same schedule: Leave England on Sunday, flying into the sun. Spend a little time with them that night and all day Monday. Then reverse course on Tuesday, flying through the dark night, then arriving in time for training on Wednesday. However sore and tired I was on those Sunday flights— the games rip you apart—I'd return feeling refueled.

The trips were worth every one of the hundreds of thousands of miles traveled, worth the jet lag and the discomfort.

I wouldn't fly halfway around the world and back to spend thirty-six hours with Elvis or the pope, or anyone else.

But my kids? Yes, I would. And I did. Every chance I got.

CHAPTER 19
WHAT EVERY KID NEEDS

DURING THE 2010 WORLD CUP, I'D HELPED THE NEW JERSEY Center for Tourette Syndrome raise $50,000 in grant funding from Pepsi. NJCTS was going to use that money to start the leadership academy that Faith Rice had planned.

More recently, I'd helped them raise more money from a raffle: Team Up with Tim Howard. The family who won the drawing would fly to England with my mom. We'd all have lunch together, and they'd catch an Everton game.

The winners were a family named the Kowalskis: Tim and Leslie and their two daughters, twelve-year-old

Tess and eight-year-old Paige.

I missed my own kids so much, I was excited for the visit. I was eager to spend time with any kids by this point!

Both Tess and Paige had been diagnosed with TS.

"Just so you know," Mom warned me, "Tess in particular has a pretty severe case."

We met at a restaurant in Liverpool. When I spotted the Kowalskis walking up to the restaurant, I thought, *This looks like one sweet family.*

I liked how gently Tim Kowalski nudged the girls forward, encouraging them to shake my hand. I liked the warmth in Leslie's voice whenever she spoke to the girls.

I could tell that Tess and Paige trusted their parents, and that the trust worked both ways. Sort of like Mom and me, I realized.

Mom and I sat on one side of the table, the Kowalskis on the other. Both Leslie and Tim encouraged the girls to come sit near me. Both shook their heads. They were sticking with Mom and Dad.

Tess and Paige both had Leslie's dark hair and sparkling eyes. They had their dad's smile. Did they fidget more than other kids their age, make more noise? Sure. But that didn't change who they were. Sweet, shy kids.

"You know, I really want to thank you for this," Leslie said to me.

I shrugged, as if to say, *No big deal.*

"No, I mean it," Leslie said. "It's been a really tough year for our family. Tess has been dealing with the strongest tics she's ever had. It's been hard for her."

She turned to Tess. "Okay if I tell him about your TS?"

When Tess nodded, her mom added, "Do you want to tell him yourself?" At this, Tess looked alarmed; her eyes said no. Mom and I exchanged a quick glance of recognition.

I remembered so well not wanting to talk about TS.

Leslie explained that Tess's symptoms had shown up in kindergarten: grunting and sniffing and throat clearing and shoulder jerks. After a while, Tess resisted going to school at all. She cried every morning. By the end of her kindergarten year, the crying had turned to screaming. When she came home with a picture she'd drawn, it was always in gray colors, stick figures with sad faces. The boys in the class were teasing her, Tess said. She couldn't stand being there.

Yup, I thought. *I know exactly what that's like, not wanting to sit through school.*

Her parents were bewildered, but they could see how sad she was.

They knew they needed to figure out what was going on. Eventually, they got a diagnosis: Tourette Syndrome.

Her symptoms had become even more noticeable

since then. For a while she spit on people. She blew in their faces.

"And sometimes I poked them in the eye," Tess added. Immediately, she clammed up again. She looked back down at the table.

Leslie reached over to rub her daughter's back. "That's true," she said. "But you couldn't help it."

"I know," Tess said. "But I wish I could."

My mom reached over to me then and touched my forearm almost unconsciously.

Tess's next symptom, Leslie said, was muttering curses under her breath.

Tim Kowalski flashed a warm smile at his daughter. "I thought, oh boy," he said. "What's coming next?"

It was so interesting the way this family talked about TS. They were so open about it.

Tess didn't seem to be ashamed by the conversation; she didn't mind her parents' comments. These were simply the facts of Kowalski family life. They talked about the trials of TS matter-of-factly, as other families might talk about hiring a math tutor.

Their openness and ease seemed really positive to me.

It's a tough world out there. It's tough for all kids, but if you've got something that makes you different from everyone else—TS or anything—it's so easy to feel ashamed. I remember feeling relieved when I realized my mom had noticed all my TS symptoms. It had helped. It had made me feel less alone, like at least here, with my mom, I didn't have to hide. What if all kids had somebody in their lives with whom they could be completely and totally themselves?

As Tess grew older, she found a way to mask the curses . . . sort of. She'd figured out that if she mumbled her curses and strung them together as fast as she could—*&%$#!—people might not understand what she was saying. If she added the word "pie" to the end of a string of curses—*&%$#!PIE—it obscured the curses even further.

My mom and I were impressed.

"That's pretty smart, Tess," Mom said.

Paige, Tess's younger sister, had been diagnosed with TS more recently. So far, the disorder manifested as grunting, whistling, and throwing her shoulder so far forward that she occasionally dislocated it. Her symptoms weren't as severe as her sister's. But I remembered how I felt when my own symptoms were labeled "mild."

When you're living inside TS, there's no such thing as mild. Whatever your symptoms, it's darned hard to cope with.

I told the Kowalskis about my own experience, especially the battle to suppress my tics. I told them that when I tried to hide my tics, I wasn't able to focus on anything going on in the classroom. I'd had a choice: tic, and learn, or hide tics, and learn nothing.

I'd chosen to hide them, and I'd learned almost nothing.

"But I don't try to hide them anymore," I said. "I just let them pass through me. As you get older, you stop worrying as much about hiding them, you know?"

"And it seems like it's never held you back," said Leslie.

"Right," I responded. "In fact, the only thing that ever held me back was attempting to hide TS." And that, I knew now, was the truth.

The Kowalskis came to Goodison Park the next day, watching as Everton beat Wolverhampton 2-1. I met them after the game and introduced them around. "This is Marouane Fellaini. Leighton Baines. Phil Jagielka." We snapped some photos of the family as they posed with players.

The Kowalskis then returned to New Jersey, and to navigating their lives with TS. I couldn't stop thinking about them after they left, remembering what Faith Rice had told me the first time we met.

These kids are going to have to stand up for themselves every day of their lives.

* * *

A few months later, I got a package from the Kowalskis. Each of the girls had written a thank-you note. Leslie had made me a hand-knitted scarf, perfect for the bitter Manchester winters.

Leslie included a note of her own:

> *Tim—*
>
> *Tess recently decided to give a talk in front of a hundred people about TS. She explained what TS was, and what it felt like to have it.*
>
> *She used you as a model of someone who lives successfully with TS.*
>
> *I don't know that she would have done that if she hadn't met you. I wish every child with TS could have the chance to sit with someone who understands them.*
>
> *Leslie*

Funny. I'd spent the last few months wishing that every child with TS could have people like the Kowalskis surrounding them.

PART FOUR

CHAPTER 20
CHANGING THE SCOREBOARD

HERE IS WHAT IT'S LIKE TO ARRIVE AT THE ESTADIO AZTECA in Mexico City—the stadium where Mexico plays.

You're wheezing, first of all. The Azteca is 7,349 feet above sea level. The air is thin. But it's hard to tell if you're short of breath because of the altitude, or the city's blanket of smog. Forget about playing a game: simply walking up a flight of stairs makes you feel like you've just climbed Kilimanjaro.

It's the greatest home field advantage I've ever encountered.

The moment the bus pulls off the highway, you can see Azteca in the distance. It's huge—114,000 seats in steep risers, and it looms over the city like some strange, mythical beast. But for the moment, all you can do is look at that stadium in the distance. There's standstill traffic everywhere, in all directions. Nobody goes anywhere for a while.

As the bus inches toward the stadium, it grows bigger and bigger. It also grows more intimidating with each passing minute.

When you finally arrive, you head downstairs . . . far downstairs. The visitors' locker room is so deep inside that stadium that it might as well be a dungeon.

You change into your warm-up gear and walk through dingy corridors looking for a stairwell. It's poorly lit down there, dank and cold. Those corridors feel like they go on forever. You don't have any idea where you are, or how much distance remains before you get to the stadium entrance.

By the time you jog out to the field to warm up, the stands are filled with green shirts. They hiss and boo and jeer when you walk out onto the grass.

All this, and you haven't even touched the ball yet.

It's intimidating. And the more times you go down there without winning, the more you feel like you *can't* win. Not there.

And for most of the US history there—nine games and zero wins—we didn't.

* * *

On August 15, 2012, when we arrived at Aztcca, our record there was 0–8–1. We were 0–23–1 in all games against Mexico on their soil.

We'd gone down there for a "friendly" match, although the US-Mexico rivalry is anything but friendly.

We had a new Team USA coach, Jürgen Klinsmann. He'd taken the helm after the 2010 World Cup. He'd made some big changes, too.

Our training regimens were different. With Bob, we'd generally had one long session each day, often filling the afternoon with discussions of tactics and videotape viewings. Jürgen had us training twice a day. Sometimes three times.

Bob had always allowed us to dress the way we wanted to dress in our free time. If we wanted to eat a chicken fajita once in a while, he let us. As long as we were at trainings on time, we could wake up when we wanted and go to sleep when we wanted.

Jürgen dictated when we woke and when we slept. He changed our diet and exercise regimens. Each dawn, we took "empty stomach runs," thirty minutes of early-morning sprints.

He wanted to mold us, shape us, push us further than we could imagine.

* * *

Jürgen had made me captain for this game. It was going to be a tough match. Many of our most experienced players—Clint Dempsey, Michael Bradley, Jozy Altidore, Carlos—wouldn't be there.

But I was going to give this game everything I had.

Down in that locker room, I moved from one player to the next, reminding them of their responsibilities. I watched as Landon laced up his cleats. He looked like he was a gladiator, about to face the lion . . . like he didn't believe he'd even be coming back.

I slid on my captain's armband. The locker room bell rang, signaling that it was time to head up to the tunnel, start lining up.

I held up my hand to the team. "No," I said. "Wait."

No one moved.

I wanted to make the Mexico players wait. I wanted them to stand there lined up in the tunnel, not sure where we were.

I wanted them to not see us coming. I wanted *them* to have to turn around to look at *us*.

After a few long moments, I led our team out into the hallway, that long, dark walk beneath the stadium, and up the concrete ramp to where the Mexican players stood.

Our voices in those corridors were deep and loud.

"Come on, boys! This is our night!"

We lined up next to the Mexican players and stared straight ahead.

I held my chin high. Tightened my jaw. Behind me, I knew all the other guys were doing the same.

If any of us felt fear about the game we were about to play, we weren't going to show it.

The first half was like a tennis match; the ball went back and forth. Neither side accomplished much. Mexico created some good chances, but at halftime, it was 0–0.

Mexico came on strong in the second half. They attacked in waves, but they didn't score.

Then, in the eightieth minute, three of our second-half substitutes—Brek Shea, Terrence Boyd, and Michael Orozco-Fiscal—changed the game. Kyle Beckerman passed to Brek, who hit a low cross to the top of the six yard box. Terrence sent the ball toward the right post.

There, Michael Orozco-Fiscal—in only his fifth appearance for the national team—kicked it in the net.

Whoa, I thought. *We're winning.*

We needed to hold that 1–0 lead for ten more minutes.

Ten minutes might sound short, but in a high-intensity game, they can feel endless. Those final minutes were as tough as any I'd ever faced on the field. Mexico was determined to get a goal. I had to make a sprawling save in the eighty-fourth minute. Five minutes later, I had to make another incredibly tough save.

But we held them.

When the final whistle blew, the crowd was stunned into almost complete silence.

The US had beaten Mexico at Azteca—something that had never happened before. Not in decades of competing against them.

The Azteca locker room was as celebratory as I've ever seen it. Even though this was technically a "friendly," the victory felt as important as any we'd ever had—as big as Spain. Or Algeria.

I remember looking across the room at Landon. He had this huge, wide smile plastered across his face. But he also looked bewildered, as if some part of him were wondering, *Is this even real? Did this really happen?*

Landon caught my eye then, and for a moment we just grinned at each other.

Yeah, it's real. It happened.

On the way out of the stadium, there's a long ramp filled with plaques. Every team that's ever played in Azteca has their record listed in the stadium.

We found ours, and we stared at it for a while. In the wins column, there was a zero.

They were going to have to change it, as a result of what we'd done here today.

I took a picture of myself with that sign, and I texted it to Mulch.

On the bus ride home, a text popped up from Mulch: *Way to represent New Jersey!*

I laughed. But I didn't reply to him right away. Instead, as we rolled slowly through Mexico City, I dialed a Memphis number.

"Hi, Tim," Laura said when she picked up.

"Hey," I said. "Guess what? We just beat Mexico. At the Azteca."

She gasped.

"Oh my goodness!" she exclaimed.

Then I heard her calling out into the house, "Jacob! Ali! Come to the phone! Your daddy just made history!"

We would meet Mexico again. We'd draw 0–0 with them at Azteca in March 2013, and six months later, we'd beat them 2–0 at a World Cup qualifier in Columbus, Ohio.

The tide was turning. Team USA was not to be dismissed.

It felt amazing.

CHAPTER 21
BROKEN

NEAR THE END OF THE 2012-2013 PREMIER LEAGUE SEASON,
Everton played Oldham Athletic on February 26, 2013, in
the FA Cup. Oldham's a lower-league team, so the game
was a big deal for them.

We were winning comfortably 3–1. Toward the end,
Oldham brought on a substitute.

I'll call this sub Bonehead, and there's a good reason
why.

From the moment Bonehead came on, he ran around
that field making rash challenges. He kicked people; he
knocked into them harder than he needed to.

It was like he'd decided, "This is a Premier League team, so I'm going to make a name for myself."

Except that isn't how it's done in the Premier League. We might be rough-and-tumble, but we play fairly.

At one point, the ball came toward me. It flew into the air toward the left-hand side of the box. It was a nothing play: jump, catch it, come down.

But while I was up in the air—the ball high over my head—Bonehead barged straight into me. There was no intent to play the ball, just me.

When Bonehead and I collided, he swept my legs out from underneath me. Ordinarily, I'd try to land on my side, shoulder, hip, or stomach. But because of my positioning, and his, I couldn't.

My back and tailbone hit the ground first.

I've had plenty of injuries in my career. I've been bumped and bruised and kicked and elbowed and knocked down again and again. I'd broken my finger back in 2007. I'd had players—like Heskey in the England game—slam into me, studs up.

This was different.

I tried to roll over, but I kept getting a sharp, shooting pain.

One of the doctors, Danny Donachie, rushed onto the field.

I lay there flat, looking at the sky. "Danny," I said. "I'm really hurt, I'm really hurt. It's my back. Danny, I'm not okay."

He asked if I could get up. I tried but couldn't step too hard on my left side without doubling over.

"Can you play?" Danny asked.

No, I can't.

"Maybe," I said.

I should have left the game then and there. But I didn't.

I couldn't.

I felt like when I was a kid, and I had to touch things in a certain order. Stopping the game before it was over felt wrong. Terribly, ominously wrong. How could I stop playing when I wasn't finished?

The ref had called a foul, awarding us a free kick from deep in our end. It would normally be my kick. But I was thinking, *I don't actually know if I can make this kick.*

The referee blew the whistle. I backed up, but I was hobbling. I stepped gingerly toward the ball, planted my left foot.

And I got this screaming pain up the left side of my back.

I kicked anyway, but I was in agony at that moment. In fact, I was in agony for the rest of the game.

The next morning, I couldn't get out of bed. It took

me five full minutes to move to a sitting position on the edge of the bed.

On Saturday, we were scheduled to play Reading. So on Friday, Chris Woods and I met early to get a sense of what I could do. But I couldn't bend down, I couldn't dive. I caught a couple of balls standing still, and that was about it.

"The game's not for twenty-four hours," I said. *Twenty-four hours is enough time to heal.* I was trying to convince myself. *I'll be better in twenty-four hours.*

But I wasn't. The morning of the game, I could barely move—couldn't possibly dive to catch a ball. How could I protect Everton's goal if I couldn't dive?

When I said the three words I'd never willingly said before—*I can't play*—I felt nauseated.

I tried to watch the game in the stands that day. I tried. But I couldn't stand seeing all the action and not being able to control any of it. I lasted maybe fifteen minutes before heading inside.

There, I watched the rest of the game with Jimmy Martin. It was just the two of us. Between the pain of my back and the frustration of not being on the field, Jimmy's grumbling was a welcome noise.

Later that week, I learned that I had two broken vertebrae.

I was in the training room with Danny when the

results came back. I heard his side of the conversation only.

"Okay, two vertebrae . . . fractured . . . right . . . and how much time should he . . . four to six . . ."

That's when I panicked. *Four to six months? I was going to have to sit out for four to six months??!*

I couldn't afford to be out of the game for that long. I'd miss important World Cup qualifiers. I'd miss the end of the season. I'd miss so much training.

I'd be a different player entirely if I stopped practicing for that long.

I'd miss, I felt sure, next year's World Cup.

I was thirty-four years old—getting older, even for a goalkeeper. If I missed this World Cup, I might not get another shot.

For a few moments, I wondered if this was the beginning of the end.

Danny hung up the phone. "Okay, Tim," he said. "You're going to need to rest for four to six weeks."

Weeks. Not months.

Relief flooded over me. Weeks I could do.

But boy, was that a wake-up call. That's how quickly it can all change. One minute, the World Cup is within your grasp. A minute later, it can all be taken away.

* * *

I went home to Memphis to recover. Laura let me spend much of that time lying on the sofa of her house. She served me food and water, and when I was well enough, she let me rummage through the refrigerator on my own.

When I came back, I played my three hundredth game for Everton. We drew 0–0. That shutout just happened to be my hundredth clean sheet.

One hundred clean sheets in three hundred games: it's a pretty darned good record for a goalkeeper. But more than the record, it felt terrific to be back out there.

Thank goodness that injury wasn't worse, I thought. *Thank goodness I can keep doing this for a while longer.*

CHAPTER 22
CHANGING FACES

There were a lot of changes happening in my life.

Not only did we have a new coach on the US National Team, I was going to get one at Everton, too.

You see, not long after I'd returned from my broken back, Sir Alex Ferguson—the head coach at Manchester United—announced that he'd be retiring after twenty-seven years at the helm.

His replacement would be David Moyes—my beloved Everton coach.

In May 2013, Moyes attended his final game as the Everton coach. In that game, we played West Ham at home.

When David arrived at Goodison, he was met with applause and cheers. The stands were filled with handmade signs: THANK YOU DAVID MOYES. When he appeared on the sideline, every fan in the stadium stood for him—a sign of respect.

After the game was over—a satisfying 2–0 win, thanks to two great goals by Kevin Mirallas—the players lined up along the edge of the field so David could walk between us, honor guard style. I swear, I couldn't imagine Goodison without him.

That summer, it was announced that Roberto Martinez, who'd been the coach at Wigan Athletic, would replace David Moyes as Everton's new head coach. Although Wigan had been in the Premier League only since 2005, Roberto had managed them well. This year, he'd taken them on a memorable FA Cup run. They even beat the heavily favored Manchester City in the final.

Roberto brought some new players to Everton— James McCarthy from Wigan; Romelu Lukaku, a Belgian international, from Chelsea; and Gareth Barry, an English international from Manchester City. Romelu and Gareth would start on one-year loans, just as I had.

I liked Roberto and all the new Everton players. I especially liked Romelu. At twenty-one, he was already a major talent. He was also as driven as any player I'd ever seen. He was hungry. In his spare time, he studied videos of the world's great strikers. He'd made a highlight reel of plays by Ronaldo, Didier Drogba, Robin van Persie, and Wayne Rooney. He relaxed with video games—soccer video games, of course.

After practice, he fired shots at me, both of us honing our skills.

He was nice, too—as decent and as down-to-earth as anyone I'd played with.

He may have just been there on loan, but he *felt* like an Evertonian.

The fans loved Romelu, too. During his first Everton game, away against West Ham, he scored the winning goal; in his Goodison debut, he'd scored two goals. Then, in the Merseyside derby, he'd scored two goals against Liverpool. It had earned us a draw, 3–3. Later, he declared the whole event to be his best experience in club soccer.

There were some changes in the US National Team player roster, too.

Landon had decided to take a break from the US National Team. He was exhausted from a decade and a half of the soccer schedule. He was tired of flying around the world and pinning his hopes on ninety minutes of play.

I understood it—that schedule was similar to my own. And I knew how much I had sacrificed to play the game. I rarely saw my mom these days, or my brother Chris, or Mulch. My marriage had ended, and I no longer got to live with my kids.

But still. I worried.

I worried about Landon's career, first of all. Take time off when you're thirty-one, and you risk never coming back—even when you're Landon Donovan.

I worried about the team, because we needed him. We had important World Cup qualifiers coming up.

And I worried, selfishly, about me—mostly because I couldn't imagine playing without him.

I picked up the phone to call Landon. I wanted to remind him how important he was to the team . . . and how important our upcoming games were.

I dialed his number, but hung up before I heard it start ringing.

Landon didn't need to hear from me. He knew the risks. I put the phone down.

On his sabbatical, Landon spent time doing all the things you can't do when you're on the soccer schedule. He took long walks with his dog. He reconnected with family and friends. He traveled to Cambodia, where he played games of pickup soccer purely for the joy of it.

It looked, actually, like he had a whole lot of fun.

And when he returned, he was refreshed. He came back from his break in time for the 2013 Gold Cup, where he stole the show. He scored five goals and earned seven assists.

To my mind, Landon proved—again—that he was still the best of the best.

The same spring, Jürgen had left Carlos off the roster for some important World Cup qualifying matches, moving in less experienced defenders. These guys weren't better; they were younger, and they were fighting hard to establish themselves and their careers.

Carlos had some long, difficult conversations with Jürgen.

It became clear: Carlos was getting phased out of the team.

It's part of what happens in every World Cup cycle, but Carlos was a dear friend, so it was hard to see. But that's soccer: your position disappears in an instant.

Already, so many of the guys I'd come up through the ranks with were gone.

Carlos faced a choice: he could sit on the bench and watch the play from the sidelines, occasionally getting called in as a sub, or he could step aside for the new generation.

He called me to ask what I thought he should do.

"What is it you want to do, Carlos?" I asked.

"I don't know, Tim. I really don't."

I remembered what it felt like when I broke my back, how agonizing it was to say "I can't play." How fearful I was in those moments when I thought the whole ride might suddenly be over.

We talked for a while. Then I said, "Carlos, you've been an incredible captain. Amazing things have happened under your leadership. Do you really think you'd want to go back to being a substitute?"

There was a long, painful silence. Then Carlos said, "I know what I need to do."

And by his voice, I understood: Carlos wasn't going to be my captain anymore. We weren't going to be teammates.

Between Landon's sabbatical and Carlos's departure from the team, I suddenly felt like the last of a generation.

It wasn't just professionally that things were changing, either.

Recently, Laura had called me up. "Tim," she said. Her voice was bubbly, warm. "I've met someone. His name is Trey."

There's the joy, I thought. There's the joy in her voice that I remember so well.

It was with the same voice that had once called her mom from a Times Square hotel to tell her we were getting married. The same voice that had overflowed with excitement when she'd purchased a wedding dress—the one she never got to wear.

The voice was unmistakable: Laura had fallen in love again.

I was happy for her. Laura deserved someone who adored her completely. I was glad for Ali and Jacob, too; it could only be good for them to see their mother joyful. If this guy, Trey, was all Laura seemed to think he was, he'd be another warm heartbeat in their lives, another source of love.

But I was a little nervous for my own sake.

What if he and I didn't click and he didn't want me around? What if he couldn't understand how important the kids were to me?

A few weeks later, I made one of my lightning-fast visits home. Laura had arranged for us all to meet up at a Memphis Grizzlies basketball game—her, me, Trey, Jacob, Ali, and Trey's two kids, Savannah and Jake.

Before the game, Laura said, "Trey wanted to make sure you knew he didn't have to come tonight. He said if you preferred to spend time with the kids without him around, he understands."

That, right there, told me everything I needed to know. Trey understood exactly how important my time with the kids was. And he was making it clear that he wasn't going to get in the way of that.

"Of course he should come," I said.

"You sure?"

"Yeah. I'd love to meet him."

When I did meet him—when I saw the way he smiled at Laura, the way he laughed so easily with his kids and my own—I knew.

I knew Trey was going to be in all of our lives for a long time.

CHAPTER 23
WORLD CUP TRAINING

JÜRGEN NAMED A THIRTY-MAN ROSTER FOR THE 2014 WORLD Cup training; since only twenty-three of us could go to Brazil, it meant we'd practice together for a few weeks . . . then he'd send seven of us home.

Carlos had retired from the team by now, so he wasn't part of the thirty.

But Landon was.

We trained at Stanford University. We ate in the dining halls, surrounded by researchers and rocket scientists, some of the smartest people on this planet.

We ran. We did our drills. We scrimmaged. We prepared.

* * *

Then, a few weeks into training, I was in the locker room, and one by one, players began to filter in. A few seemed distraught.

One sat down and began to cry.

And that's when I realized: this was the day Jürgen was making cuts. One by one, Jürgen was quietly sending seven guys home.

The locker room got very still.

A player who didn't make the cut sat down on the floor, head in hands. He couldn't even bear to look at anyone.

One of the other guys threw things against the wall.

Then Landon walked into the locker room.

I could tell immediately. It was something about how he held his head. It seemed impossible, and yet I knew without a shred of doubt: Landon wasn't going to the World Cup.

I remembered, in that moment, seeing him when he scored his first professional goal against me in 2001. We'd grown up together, as players and as men. I'd watched Landon handle the pressure of being a young prodigy, a young superstar. We'd been together for so many big moments.

We'd been together when we beat Mexico in 2007 in

the Gold Cup. We'd been together when we beat Mexico on their soil. We'd been together when we beat Spain in the Confederations Cup. We'd been together in South Africa. He'd even come to Everton to play in the off-season a couple times.

We'd traveled the globe together, experienced wild highs and deep lows. Now I was going to have to go to Brazil, to the World Cup, without him.

He said just three words to the team.

"I'm going home."

Some of the guys spoke to him. They told him how sorry they were, told him that they couldn't believe it.

I didn't say anything at all.

I knew my words would have rung hollow. Landon wasn't yet in a place where words were going to mean anything.

Besides, Landon knew. He knew exactly how I felt about him.

A few of us on the World Cup squad had a lot of experience—DaMarcus Beasley and Clint Dempsey had more than one hundred caps. Michael Bradley and I had nearly one hundred. But many on the team were brand-new—Julian Green, who'd grown up in Germany, was still a teenager, and had just three caps. John Brooks, another American raised in Germany, had five. Between us, only two players had ever scored in a World Cup: Clint had scored twice, and Michael Bradley once. Of the twenty-three guys who were going to Brazil, seventeen were heading to their first World Cup.

Scanning the roster, I realized that some of these guys were closer in age to Jacob than they were to me.

It's funny how quickly a person can go from being an upstart to part of an old generation. It had happened in the blink of an eye.

But that's what happens: experience is replaced by youth.

We'd been placed into the so-called "Group of Death"—the toughest of all eight groups. We'd open with Ghana, the team that had knocked us out of the round of sixteen in the last World Cup. They had also helped send us home in 2006.

We'd play Portugal, where we'd face the newly crowned World Player of the Year, Cristiano Ronaldo.

We'd play Germany—the team I was betting would win the whole thing.

Plus, our matches would require nearly nine thousand miles of travel, including a visit to Manaus, a city deep in the Amazonian jungle, which was known for its steamy and strength-sapping weather conditions.

Jürgen called our draw "the worst of the worst."

* * *

Right before we left for the World Cup and twelve years after I played my first senior game for the United States, I received my hundredth cap, this one against Nigeria. The game was held in Jacksonville, Florida, on June 7. Laura brought the kids down. Friends and family from all over came to watch: My agent, Dan, was there. Mulch. Some of my high school buddies. My brother, Chris, hadn't been able to make it—he and his girlfriend had recently had a baby girl—but aside from him, it was almost everybody who mattered in my life. I'd never had all these people in the same place, at the same time.

I was just the fifteenth player in US history to reach the hundred-cap mark. I now held the team record for wins as a goalkeeper. One hundred games. If I tried, I couldn't possibly recount them all—many had faded into a blur.

I was thirty-five years old, the oldest player on the World Cup squad.

US Soccer made me a jersey with the number 100.

I held it up for photographs, and then brought my family onto the field—me, my mom and dad, my beautiful kids.

I cherish the pictures from that day. The stands are filled. My teammates are off to my side. My dad is on my right, with his hand on Jacob. My mom is on my left, and my arm is around her, tight. And in front of all of us is

Ali. She and her brother are holding up that commemorative jersey.

HOWARD

100

All those games I'd played. All those friends I'd made and kept along the way. Nearly all of them there with me—minus, of course, Landon and Carlos.

After the game, I signed my jersey and gave it to Mulch.

Mulch:
We did it.
I love you.
Tim

He gave me a long, long hug. He was still the same guy I'd known since I was fifteen. He still had the same fire, the same intensity.

He was the man who made me who I am, and he was rooting for me as hard as he ever had.

Then he said, "Go win."

Right after the game, we flew to Brazil.

CHAPTER 24
TEAM USA

OUR WORLD CUP TEAM HAD PLAYERS WHO HAD BEEN BORN and raised overseas. For some of the new members of our squad, English wasn't their first language. At one point I realized that some of the Americans who'd been raised abroad didn't know our national anthem. John Brooks, for example, had no idea what the words were.

I liked John. He was quiet and humble, and at just twenty-one years old, he was already a great defender. John and I spent a lot of time together on the field, and we often roomed together—the old man and the new kid on the block, just as Tony Meola and I had once been.

"You don't know the national anthem?" I asked. I

couldn't believe it! "Well, that's going to change."

I got ahold of some printouts of "The Star-Spangled Banner." I handed them out during a team meal. "Learn this," I said. "You've got a few days, and then we'll all sing it together."

Over the next few days, I checked in with these guys: "Have you learned it yet? You ready to sing?"

When we finally sang it together toward the end of training, I suddenly understood how lucky it is that our voices are usually drowned out by fifty thousand fans.

We sounded horrendous.

But I'll tell you: during the national anthem before our Ghana game, the first of our World Cup matches, I glanced over to the sidelines. I looked to the place where John Brooks stood with the other subs.

He was singing proudly. Every word.

Ghana was the team that had sent us home in 2010. They also played a role in our going home in 2006. A lot of my teammates were so young, they probably didn't remember 2006, maybe couldn't have even told you the score.

But I remembered all of it.

Now, in 2014, we couldn't have imagined a better start to the Ghana match. Thirty-one seconds in, Clint Dempsey settled the ball off a throw-in from Jermaine Jones. Clint surged toward Ghana's goal. He blew past two defenders.

Then he steered a low shot inside the far post.

1–0 and the game wasn't even a minute old.

But the game was a tough one—so tough that three of our players were injured.

First, Jozy dropped to the ground. He clutched his hamstring—it would turn out to be a serious tear, one that would keep him out the rest of the tournament. Then, right before halftime, Matt Besler pulled *his* hamstring. He was replaced by John Brooks.

Clint Dempsey broke his nose in an aerial collision. Clint's a leader and a fighter, though: he stuffed his nose full of cotton and played on.

In the second half, we defended like crazy, and we held them off until the eighty-second minute. Then Ghana scored, and it was 1–1.

We didn't want a draw. We were in such a tough group—still with Portugal and Germany ahead. If we didn't win this one, we might not advance at all.

In the eighty-sixth minute, we got a corner kick. John Brooks, our young, anthem-singing, German-born sub, soared above everyone else in the box. He headed the ball—a perfect downward shot into the goal.

It was a heart-stopping moment, one of those last-gasp miracles.

You could see that Brooks barely believed what had just happened. He scrambled toward the edge of the field and just lay there, facedown.

Later, he'd tell us that he'd dreamed about this moment—actually dreamed, while sleeping, that he scored a game-winning goal in the eightieth minute of the Ghana game.

He was off by a few minutes, but nobody was about to quibble.

USA 2, Ghana 1.

Laura brought the kids down to cheer me on. In the days before the Portugal game, the kids and I swam in the hotel pool and played video games. Sometimes all the children of Team USA would get together for a game of hallway soccer outside the media room. In those games, I stood on my knees as a goalkeeper, letting Michael Bradley's toddler son—like a mini-Michael, just with more hair—kick the ball past me.

Ali was on my team, and she was endlessly frustrated with my play in the hallway matches.

"Daddy," she scolded. She was furious. "You have to *stop* the ball!"

By the time we got to the Portugal game, they looked like a wounded animal. They had been humiliated 4–0 by Germany in their opening match. During that match, their central defender, Pepe, had been sent off the field for head-butting a German player, Thomas Müller. That meant he would miss this game.

Cristiano Ronaldo would be there. Although he was reported to be carrying an injury, I knew: even injured, Cristiano is pretty much unstoppable.

We worked long and hard on a game plan to slow him down. Our plan was to funnel him into areas where he'd do the least damage.

Portugal scored early, but if history had taught us anything, it was that we could fight back from early deficits. Soon after we went down 1–0, we hit our stride. We played the best soccer that we played in the tournament. We moved the ball crisply and cleanly. Clint Dempsey and Michael Bradley both forced the Portugal keeper into sprawling saves to preserve their lead.

Meanwhile, you couldn't even tell Ronaldo was on the field, he was so quiet.

We were still down 1–0 at the half, but in the sixty-fourth minute we broke through. Jermaine Jones sent a rocket through a packed box. He scored one for our side.

Game on.

Then Clint scored again, ten minutes from the end.

I thought we had it won. Judging by the roar that shook the stadium, our fans thought so, too.

You can never count out the great players, though. They can always make something special happen as long as there are still seconds on the clock.

There were.

Michael lost the ball in midfield, and Cristiano Ronaldo pounced.

Cristiano propelled a ball over our defense. His kick was inch-perfect—just far enough out of my reach that the Portuguese striker Varela could head in an equalizer in the final seconds of the game. It was practically the last touch before the game's end.

Cristiano had been barely noticeable all game. Then, with just seconds to go, he came up with that piece of artistry. Only a few players in the world could have pulled that off. We were numb as we walked off the field. We'd had everything we'd wanted in our grasp. We'd thought we had the win. We'd thought for sure we were going to advance. Then, in the final seconds, it was taken away.

Mind you, 2–2 is not a bad result against a team of Portugal's pedigree . . . except when you thought you had them beat.

But as sad as I felt, I knew that Ali, Jacob, and Laura were in the stands, about to return to Memphis. This was my last chance to catch a glimpse of them before they went home.

In the locker room, I stripped down to my shorts and T-shirt. I put my running shoes on and returned to the field. I waved to them, blew kisses, and pretended to catch their kisses back. We had as much fun as we could, given the distance between their seats and the grass.

When it was time for them to head to the airport for the trip back to Memphis, I blew them one final kiss— just the latest in our countless good-byes—and began to think about Germany.

The night before the Germany game, there had been a virtual monsoon in Recife, where we were playing. Overnight, rain had turned roads into rivers. As we drove toward the stadium, we were informed that the buses taking friends and families from our hotel to the match might not be able to make it there. Apparently, our loved ones had been given a choice: they could remain in the hotel and be guaranteed the opportunity of seeing the game on television. Or they could take their chances and possibly get stuck on the bus en route.

My mom, who was there for the duration of the tournament, stayed at the hotel.

My dad, who'd flown down for this game only, boarded the bus.

The bus never made it. Actually, even with police escorts, *our* bus barely made it.

The rain was so bad we weren't even allowed a warm-up on the field, for fear we'd wreck the turf before the opening whistle.

* * *

Long before this game, I knew that Germany was the best team in the tournament. I could see it in how they played; they had skill, fitness, and remarkable tactical smarts.

They were as close to perfect as there was.

Fortunately, we didn't need to beat them to advance; a draw would automatically get us through. It was even possible that we'd qualify for the knockout round with a loss. We had a slim margin over Ghana based on goal differential. As long as we could preserve that, we could still advance.

Ghana would be playing Portugal as we played Germany. I wanted to know the score of that game, because I wanted to adjust my strategy. If, based on that other game, we absolutely needed a goal to advance, I could push one of my fullbacks forward, take more risks.

But if we might get through even without a goal, I could tuck players in, hold them back, and concentrate on not letting Germany score on us.

From the kickoff, Germany attacked relentlessly. They were an absolute machine. Because Germany always seemed to have the ball, that meant I had a busy forty-five minutes. I was called on to make a couple of tough saves, but for the most part our defense held firm. At halftime, the game remained scoreless.

Then, in the fifty-fifth minute, the big German

defender Per Mertesacker took a shot. The best I could do was parry it to the edge of the box. There, Thomas Müller was waiting. He ripped a grass-cutter past me into the far corner. I sprawled for it, but unless I was made of elastic, there was no getting that one.

Now Germany was up 1–0.

I glanced at Chris Woods then. He held up both index fingers. He was telling me that a thousand miles away, Portugal and Ghana were tied, 1–1.

If Ghana scored again, and if our score remained the same, we'd be going home.

In the seventy-third minute, two of our players, Jermaine Jones and Alejandro Bedoya, collided with each other during an aerial challenge. I could hear the smack of their heads from where I stood, half a field away. They both crumpled to the ground. Jermaine lay there for two full minutes. Later we'd learn that he'd broken his nose, just like Clint had—our second broken nose in three games.

With ten minutes left, Chris flashed me a 2–1 score with his fingers. But he didn't say whether Ghana or Portugal was winning. I glanced at Matt Besler. *Who? Who's winning?* Matt gave the tiniest shake of his head, as if to say, *Don't ask me.*

I turned back to Chris. He gave the thumbs-up sign. Portugal was ahead.

All we had to do now to advance was not to concede another goal. That is, if the Portugal/Ghana scoreboard didn't change.

We played it tight until the final whistle. It was the best we could do. There was the tiniest pause. No one was 100 percent sure of the result of the Portugal game. Then suddenly the subs and coaches on the bench started breaking toward the field at top speed. We'd just lost this game, but it was clear from their faces what the result of the other game was.

Even Woodsy—the most stoic, even-keeled man on this planet, came toward me with his arms wide.

Portugal 2, Ghana 1. We would advance.

It's funny how our Portugal tie felt so much like a loss, and how our Germany loss felt like a win.

Soccer's a complicated sport sometimes.

My mom and I went out to dinner before the Belgium game, just the two of us. It was a landmark restaurant in the lush Jardins district of São Paulo, built around a magnificent old fig tree. The restaurant was crowded.

I heard whispers. *Tim Howard . . . goalie . . . yeah, that's him.*

"Everyone here seems to know you," Mom said.

I shrugged. I was sensing a level of recognition I hadn't had yet outside of England. Even during the meal, a number of people came over to ask for autographs or photos.

Mom and I sat together for a long time. We talked about the tournament, about the children. We talked about the leadership academy that Faith Rice was planning. She'd recently announced that it would bear my name.

We talked about what life might look like for me in a few years—a world when I was done with soccer—when I finally moved to Memphis.

Mom sighed. "It's hard to believe that you might retire someday," she said. "I can't imagine you doing anything else."

"I'm thirty-five now, Mom."

She shook her head like she couldn't quite make sense of that.

We heard the *clink, clink* of silverware on plates, the murmur of fellow diners. From far away, we heard Brazilian music floating through the air. Above us, stars twinkled. I wondered how different the night sky would look to Ali and Jacob. I wondered what they were doing at that very moment.

I smiled at my mom. This was the most relaxed, undistracted time we'd had together—just the two of us—in years.

It was as if we were right back in one of those roadside

motels in Jersey: just me and Mom, eating our PB&Js. It was like nothing had changed, even though everything had.

I'd spent the years since then traveling this globe, logging more miles than I could have possibly imagined as a kid. It had been so long since Mom and I had had this kind of time together. Even sitting there, I knew it would probably be years before this could happen again.

"How do you feel about Belgium?" my mom asked.

I thought about it long and hard. And I gave her my honest answer.

"I think it's going to be a tough game," I said. "But they're certainly beatable."

CHAPTER 25
MAKING HISTORY

SO MUCH HAS BEEN SAID ABOUT THE BELGIUM GAME. EVERY minute of play has been discussed and dissected. Every save I made has been analyzed and evaluated again and again.

Since July 2, 2014, I've looked at something like eight million images of the game.

I've also seen still photos and video clips of people watching: my family, the crowd in Soldier Field, various celebrities, President Obama . . . even Landon.

I've seen pictures of strangers clutching their heads in anguish. People peeking through their fingers, or squinting through mostly closed eyes. They look like they're afraid of what they might see, yet they cannot look away.

I've seen the images from packed stadiums and crowded living rooms and city squares.

This was the game of my life, everyone said. My pinnacle moment. But it's so hard to connect all those images to what I experienced on the field.

For me, that game was both an instant and an eternity. It was all-out war, and it was just another day at my very strange office.

Here's what I would tell someone about the first ninety minutes of that game: We fought hard in the first half. We held our own. Nobody scored. Then, ten minutes into the second half, something shifted. It was like the Belgium players got a turbo boost during halftime. Suddenly, every time I looked up, a ball hurtled toward me. Mertens took shots. Fellaini. De Bruyne. Origi. Vertonghen. De Bruyne again. Vertonghen again.

I had no idea how many shots I was saving.

I knew just one thing: the score was 0–0, and it was still anybody's game.

When regulation time ended and we headed into overtime, two fifteen-minute halves, I still believed that we would win.

I believed we would find a way.

* * *

Every game a person plays is a culmination of all the experiences leading up to that moment. That was true for me in the Belgium game.

There were saves I made that felt like I was back on the fields of New Jersey. It's like I was fifteen again, back working with Mulch, playing in youth games. I was a good athlete then, but still raw. My moves back then weren't precise yet. To make a save, I had to use every part of my body: my feet, my shins, my knees, my finger-tips, my arms, my chest . . . whatever it took.

The entire second half felt like I was back in my MetroStars days. We were pinned back, just like I'd been in Giants Stadium. Everything in front of me was chaos, confusion, the way it had so often been on the losing-est team in the MLS.

In another save, De Bruyne hit a shot off a pass. I dropped down, used my body to cushion it. The ball pinged off my body before I caught it. That one? Pure Edwin Van der Sar—it was one of the moves I'd picked up by watching him.

But that sense of culmination wasn't just present in the saves I made—it was in who I was, and who was still with me.

In a way, Mulch was with me on that field. It sure felt like he was there. All those times when the shots flew in at me so fast, I didn't have time to think. All those times he fired one rocket at me after the next. The times he made me get up and keep going, when I felt like I had nothing left to give.

Tony Meola was on that field with me, too—his brash, gutsy fearlessness. And Kasey Keller—the assuredness I'd learned from him, that refusal to get rattled. My Everton coaches and teammates were there, too—in the confidence I felt, my desire to take risks.

I could keep going. If pressed, I could tell you how Landon was out there with me, and Carlos, and Bob Bradley, and Chris Woods.

And of course, my family. Isn't one's family always present, in ways both seen and unseen, in everyone's big moments?

My nana and poppa and momma and mom: they were my first coaches, the ones who modeled what it is to keep getting up again and again, to have faith in the future, no matter what's come before. And Laura and my children especially. They were present in the urgency I felt.

There had been so much sacrifice on all our parts. I'd given up everything to be on this field. I'd lost my marriage, my presence in the day-to-day lives of Ali and Jacob.

In this moment, on the world's biggest stage, I was determined to make those sacrifices worthwhile.

All game, I kept waiting to see Romelu Lukaku get off the Belgium bench. Big Rom had been a game changer at Everton last season.

He was about to become one here as well.

He subbed in for Origi at the start of extra time. His impact was instant. Matt Besler lost his balance, and Rom snatched the ball from him. Rom burst down the right wing. He spotted De Bruyne making a run into the middle of the penalty area, then crossed the ball.

It deflected off a defender and fell to the Belgian winger.

Besler had recovered from his upfield slip by now. He'd hustled down to this end and did his darnedest to block De Bruyne's shot from one direction.

In the box, I slid in from the other direction.

De Bruyne's angle was perfect, though. It flashed through the crack between our legs—that narrow tunnel that lay exactly beyond where Besler could stop it and where I could.

And now we were down by a goal. 1–0.

Now we had nothing to lose. We had everything to gain.

Everything shifted.

* * *

We pushed for the equalizer. We surged up the field. We had a great chance when Jermaine blasted a shot from the edge of the penalty area. The ball deflected off a Belgian player, and it bounced toward Clint in front of the goal.

A couple of inches to Clint's left or right, and he would have buried it. But the ball landed awkwardly under his feet. He couldn't get a shot off before Belgium cleared.

By this point, Rom was causing havoc down at our end of the field. Twice, I had to scramble the ball away from his low, hard drives.

But I could do nothing about his third attempt.

That one came in the last minute before the extra-time half.

De Bruyne flew down the left wing. He passed the ball effortlessly through our defenders. Romelu was right there; he never even broke stride as he fired the ball past me.

It went in.

Now we were down 2–0, with just a single fifteen-minute half left in the game.

I looked up in the stands then, up at my mom. The look on her face was one I rarely saw. It was a look of anguish. Poor Mom had been riding the crazy emotion of this game with me—actually, she'd been riding the crazy emotion of my *life* with me.

That second goal had clearly devastated her.

I flashed her a tiny smile. I pumped my fist slightly. It's like I was saying to her, *It's okay, Mom. It's going to be all right.*

It felt like we'd reversed roles since those youth soccer days, back when Mom watched from the sidelines.

The thing is, even if the rest of the world had given up hope, I still believed.

Back in November 2008, when I was still a fresh face at Everton, we played a game against West Ham. We'd been down by a goal until the eighty-third minute. Then, with just a few minutes left in the game, Everton's Louis Saha crossed to Joleon Lescott, who headed in an equalizer. Two minutes later, Saha drove the ball into the lower corner of the net. Then, in the eighty-seventh minute, Saha scored again. Three goals in four minutes.

That match is just one example of many. I knew that games could turn around fast, especially when teams got nervous.

If we could score just one against Belgium— take it from a comfortable lead to an uncomfortable lead—Belgium was going to get nervous. And then we could turn the game around.

Could we do it? Yeah. We could.

I really believed that, too. After all, the one defining characteristic of the US team is this: we don't give up until the final second of the clock.

After the extra-time half, Julian Green, a teenage sub on Team USA, came on the field.

Michael Bradley dinked a ball over the top of the Belgian defense. Julian took his first-ever World Cup touch.

But one touch was all it took.

Whoa, baby! Julian scored on a gorgeous volley.

At that point, nobody cared that the person who kicked it in was a teenager, a sub. Nobody thought about the fact that it was his first touch in the tournament. All that mattered was that the goal came from a white jersey.

We needed just one more. Then we could take it to a penalty kick shoot-out.

And then the siege was on the Belgium side. *We* put the pressure on *them*.

I remember looking at Michael Bradley during those final minutes. I don't think I've ever seen anyone battling harder.

Michael's engine never stops. Somehow, he'll open up into a sprint even when he's cramping. He'll push from one end of the field to the other, even when everyone around him is gasping for air. I saw Michael running. He was emptied out, I could see that. But he was still going. It's like he was fueled by hope alone.

When I saw that, I believed—not hoped, not prayed, *believed*—we were going to nail one more goal. When we did, this game would go to penalty kicks.

And if it went to PKs, I was going to do what I've done so many times before. I was going to save some. And we were going to win this thing.

And then . . . well . . . we didn't.

We had two final chances, two beautiful almosts. But the Belgian keeper was world-class. He was capable of world-class saves. We didn't score.

The whistle blew.

And that was it. After all that hope, all that heart.

We lost.

Before I knew it, Romelu was standing next to me.

He wrapped his arms around me in a hug. I've had a lot of bittersweet hugs in my life. This one just about topped them all.

Can you be happy for a friend for the exact same thing that devastates you? Yes. It turns out you can. That's a strange thing about soccer. You have your club team, and your national team. That means teammates are sometimes your opponents. Your enemy on the field might also be your dear friend.

I hugged Rom hard.

As I left the field, a FIFA official approached me. He told me something that I couldn't quite make sense of in that moment.

Truth is, I still can't quite make sense of it today.

He told me I'd just made history. That I was the first keeper to have made fifteen saves in a World Cup.

Fifteen saves.

The number was meaningless, divorced completely from this hollowed-out moment.

And history?

I shrugged. I'd have given up that World Cup history in a nanosecond if we could have made it through to the quarterfinals.

I called the kids after leaving Salvador.

"Daddy?" Ali asked in her sweet seven-year-old voice. "Are you sad?"

"Yeah," I said. "I am."

She thought about that for a bit, then responded, with more assurance than you'd think a seven-year-old could muster, "Well, I'm proud of you, Daddy. And I'm really happy. Because now you're coming home."

Just like that, I felt a little better, too.

CHAPTER 26
GAME OF MY LIFE

OVER THE NEXT FEW DAYS, I RECEIVED HUNDREDS OF TEXTS, emails, and phone calls from all over the world.

From Mulch: *You inspired a heck of a lot of kids out there today.*

I heard from Tony Meola and Kasey Keller. Landon and Carlos. Faith. I heard from high school friends and coaches. People I'd known back in Jersey, and friends I'd made in Memphis.

I was too drained, too down, to respond to more than a handful.

But I responded to Mulch with just a single word:

Gutted.

* * *

That night I slept for sixteen hours straight. In the morning, I met Clint Dempsey. We took a call from President Obama.

"You guys did us proud," the president said. Then he said to me, specifically, "I don't know how you are going to survive the mobs when you come back home, man."

Even before I left Brazil—and then for weeks after—I started getting media requests: *Jimmy Kimmel*, *The Tonight Show*, *Today*, *Dr. Oz*, *Nickelodeon Kids Choice Sports Awards*, *Good Morning America*, and the ESPYs, just to name a few.

Disney wanted to fly me to Orlando.

The ESPYs were willing to send a private jet for me and the whole family. Some places were willing to pay me lots of money—like, staggering amounts of money—if I was willing to show up, sign autographs, pose for photos.

I didn't want to do any of those appearances, though.

I wanted to go back to Memphis. I wanted to be with my kids.

The day after the game, a friend said, "Oh, goodness, Tim. You've got to see this."

It turned out that "Things Tim Howard Could Save" memes were popping up all over the internet—Photoshopped images of me "saving" disasters.

There I was, saving the *Titanic*. Saving a swimmer from the shark in *Jaws*.

She also showed me a screenshot for the Wikipedia page of the secretary of defense of the United States: someone had briefly substituted my name and image for the real one, Chuck Hagel.

Then Chuck Hagel actually called to congratulate me.

Things like that went on and on. Even months later, someone would forward me an image of graffiti, scrawled on the wall of a divorce attorney's office: TIM HOWARD COULD HAVE SAVED MY PARENTS' MARRIAGE.

It all seemed so absurd. I couldn't process any of it.

Only when I saw a *New York Times* graphic showing all fifteen saves superimposed onto a single image did the number itself make sense. I studied them in turn.

Oh yeah, I'd think. I remember that one. And that one, too.

My flight from Brazil back to the US landed at six o'clock a.m., just as the summer sun began its rise above the horizon.

It didn't occur to me at the time that walking through this airport would be any different from the hundreds of times I had walked through airports in my career.

But as soon as we got into the terminal, I quickly realized that this would be like no other stroll to baggage claim that I had ever experienced. President Obama was right. There were mobs.

I was immediately surrounded by strangers—people of every age, every background, every shape and size.

They gave me high fives. They crowded in for selfies—too many for me to count. They asked for my autograph on their boarding passes and coffee-shop receipts.

"Captain America!" shouted one middle-aged woman.

"I'm gonna grow a beard just like you!" shouted a college-aged kid, dressed in jeans and flip-flops. "You're the man!"

"Tim Howard!"

"Great game!"

"We're so proud of you!"

"Game of your life!"

I heard that phrase again and again: *Game of your life.*

Was it?

What I did on the field against Belgium is the same thing I've done in every other game throughout my career: I tried to keep the ball from going into the net.

It's what I do. Some games I barely touch the ball. I focus for ninety intense minutes, only to make one big save.

Other days, like when we played Belgium, I am asked to deliver fifteen of them.

And okay, so I made history on that field in Salvador. It didn't feel like winning in Azteca, or defeating Spain in the Confederations Cup. It's not like there were last-minute heroics like the Algeria match in South Africa.

I didn't feel elated, like when I beat Manchester United on PKs.

Slowly, it dawned on me. Over the following days I began to understand. In this game, people saw something that mattered to them. They saw something that mattered even more than winning.

They'd seen us fight, and keep fighting. We'd been knocked down and battered. We'd been bruised and depleted. Yet we'd kept going.

It wasn't just me. Every one of my teammates fought just as hard as I had. All over America, other people were fighting that hard in their own way My mom had fought that hard her whole life. My nana and poppa and momma, too. Faith Rice fought like that, and so did the Kowalskis and every kid with TS.

So many people fight. In so many ways.

But this fight had been televised in front of tens of millions of Americans. And because I was the keeper, the last man standing, I'd become the face of that fight.

That's when I understood. I might have done in the

Belgium game the same thing that I did week in, week out.

But this *had* been the game of my life.

Because in the end, maybe the game of your life simply means the one that most inspires other people.

It was a busy summer. I visited Carlos Bocanegra, my old teammate and friend, in Los Angeles. He'd just had a baby boy, and I was able to be there for the baptism.

I was the child's godfather.

It was such an honor—an honor that he asked, that Carlos wanted me to have a role in his family's life for years to come.

And I was grateful to be there.

I'd missed so many moments during the years—weddings and funerals and births and baptisms. But this one: this one I was able to attend.

The night before the baptism, Carlos told me that he was nearing the end of his MLS career. A few months later, he would announce his retirement.

Already, Carlos was staring at life beyond the soccer field.

One of these days, I would do the same.

For a few days, I got to share in his world and see a little bit about what that life might look like.

* * *

Weeks after Belgium, I opened the door to Laura and Trey's house.

"Hey, is anybody here?"

Immediately, I was surrounded by the greeting committee—the four huge dogs who share their lives with Laura and Trey and the kids. Clayton was among them, that old silly hound, wagging his tail in circles. The years were wearing on Clayton—his fur was gray, and he'd slowed down considerably, but there was no mistaking it: he was the same slobbery dog who'd caused so much mischief in our Manchester United house a decade ago.

"Okay, guys," I said, reaching down to pet Clayton. "Come on, let me through."

Trey's daughter, Savannah, greeted me first with a hug.

"Hey, Tim," she said. "Dad's in the garage. Laura's in the kitchen."

Then Ali came charging into the room. She leaped into my arms. *Man, she's getting so tall now, so grown up.*

I carried her into the kitchen. Laura was loading dishes in the dishwasher—four kids make an awful lot of dishes. "Hey, Tim."

Just last night, Ali and I had gone out to dinner, and she'd asked, "Can Mommy join us?"

"Let's ask," I'd answered. I'd texted Laura, and she

and Trey got there in time to join us for dessert.

Jacob ran into the kitchen from outdoors; at nine, he's already all limbs and angled muscles. "Hey, Dad. Can Jake sleep over tomorrow?" Jake is Trey's son.

Of course he could.

Then Trey came in. "Hey, man," he said. We clasped hands and came in for a friendly half hug.

Trey rumpled Ali's hair. "Hey, Ali. Give your dad that picture, will you?"

Ali ran over to the table and picked up a picture she'd made. It was done in Magic Marker: a green field, with a crisscross net at one end. There were two players on the field—near-stick figures with different-colored clothing, a ball between them. The player in front of the goal had his foot against the ball. She'd written the words "no goal" above him. All over the sky, she'd added the words "USA! USA! USA!"

"This one's going on my refrigerator for sure," I said.

And it did.

In August, the first-ever session of the Tim Howard NJCTS Leadership Academy kicked off in New Jersey.

Although by the time it opened I was already heading back to England, I got updates from my mom, from Faith, from people we knew in common.

Over four days, twenty-three kids with TS were

led by eight coaches—who all also had TS. One of those coaches was Marisa Lenger, the girl who'd once approached me at a MetroStars TS event with the quip, "Nice haircut."

By now, Marisa was almost thirty. Since I'd met her, she'd graduated from NYU, learned five languages, lived in Paris, risen rapidly through the ranks of an international concierge business, gotten a master's degree from American University in Paris, become the first-ever graduate speaker there, then started her own company.

I couldn't think of a better coach, a better model, for all these kids.

Later, Faith Rice described for me a single moment from the Academy—a five-minute period when all participants, both coaches and kids, started having tics at the same time.

There was whirring and hooting and echoing and roaring.

There was shoulder jerking and neck rolling and eye rolling.

There were outbursts of laughter and yelps and every noise under the sun.

After a while, it began to feel like everyone was volleying their tics, sending these noises back and forth like a Ping-Pong game.

The room was so loud that nobody could hear a word anyone else was saying.

Faith looked around at all these kids. *This,* she thought, *is the most glorious noise I have ever heard.*

At last—here, at least—these kids were free to be 100 percent themselves.

When the kids all noticed her cracking up, they burst out laughing, too.

I was happy for those kids, and a little jealous too. I wished that when I was a teenager I had been surrounded by people who understood me, who knew just what I was going through. I wish we could have laughed together about our funny brains.

Faith gave me updates on other people, too. Her son, Kim—the first person I ever met with TS—just finished his fourteenth year at his clerk position at the county courthouse. He was happy and settled, surrounded by friends.

And Tess Kowalski—the shy girl who'd visited in England in 2011—had just turned fifteen.

After that first presentation she'd done, Tess had started doing more. By now, she'd delivered lectures all over New Jersey.

She'd led teacher trainings and trainings for school administrators. She'd even visited Yale Medical School, where she presented to future physicians.

And at fifteen years old, she was just getting started.

I've gotten letters and emails from kids with TS for many years.

I've read them all. Sometimes I can't respond personally, but every one has touched me.

If I could sit down with these kids, I know exactly what I would say:

The fact that you're writing to me means you're a step ahead of where I was at your age.

You're living with TS more openly than I was. In that way, you inspire me.

Trust yourself exactly as God made you. Let your tics pass over you without fear or shame. Let them lead you along your own extraordinary journey.

It's true what that doctor told my mother all those years ago: Tourette comes with its own beautiful flip side. It gives you gifts. Mine was soccer, goalkeeping. You have something, too.

The world will not always understand. I can promise you that.

But your TS gives you a window into people's hearts. You know, better than anyone, that what lies on a person's surface isn't the thing that's real and true about them.

The thing that's real and true is never the thing on the surface.

TS helped me to understand that, too.

Your brain is extraordinary. You are extraordinary.

Everything—I promise you, everything—is possible.

In early August I returned to England. Back to the home in Manchester that Jacob and Ali and Laura and Clayton and I once shared together.

My next Premier League season was about to begin.

EPILOGUE

LIVERPOOL, UK, AUGUST 23, 2014

I'M STANDING IN THE TUNNEL, READY TO STEP ONTO THE FIELD at Goodison Park.

Prayer for my kids.

Pray they'll be safe. Pray they'll know how much I love them.

The "Z-Cars" theme begins playing, and the team begins walking.

Don't touch the "Home of the Blues" sign. Do touch the field. Make a cross.

When I see the home crowd—all those blue scarves flying—I realize how long it feels since I've been here.

It's the first home game of Everton's 2014–15 season. We're playing Arsenal, the first team I'd ever played in the league, more than a decade ago.

I've accomplished a lot in those years. There's still so much more I want to accomplish.

I made a hard decision this summer, one of the hardest of my career: I decided to take a year off playing for the US Team. For two decades, I've trained daily, crisscrossed the world again and again, gone straight from intense Premier League seasons into intense US training and tournaments. Then back again.

I have always believed that the game is a gift. It's not to be squandered. But Ali and Jacob: they are gifts, too, and I've already missed so much of their lives.

I plan to take care of myself. Work hard. Maybe, if I do it right, if all goes well, I'll have one more World Cup in me. Maybe I've still got a chance to take the US to the quarterfinals.

But I'm beginning to envision a life beyond soccer.

This summer, I signed a contract with NBC to broadcast Premier League games on television. Sometimes I think about coaching. It's a tantalizing idea—especially now that I'd be able to do great things in my home country.

There are twice as many MLS teams as there were in my MetroStars days. The MLS is attracting bigger players from around the world, keeping some of the best

Behind me, in the stands, someone shouts, "Come on, Blue Boys!"

I smile. I make one final cross over my chest.

The whistle is about to blow.

GLOSSARY

Box – the penalty area in front of and around the goal.

Cap – a term used for a player's appearance in an international game for his country.

Center back – a defensive player who primarily covers players in the middle of the field.

Clean sheet – a game in which the opposing team doesn't score on the other team.

Clearance – when a player clears the ball out of danger from his team's goal.

Corner kick – a free kick that is taken from one of the corner flags nearest to the opposing team's goal when a defender knocks the ball out of bounds over the goal line.

Danger zone – the area around the goal where most shots are scored.

homegrown players here. Attendance averages eighteen thousand per game—better than last season's NBA and NHL averages.

Whatever I choose, the number one thing I want is time.

Someday, I want to wake up in the morning and see an entire day—a line of days—during which I can be there, wholly and completely for my kids. I want to drive Ali and Jacob to school and soccer practice and basketball practice and horseback-riding lessons. I want to stand on the sidelines of their games—every one of their games—and cheer for them, the way they cheered at so many of mine.

In the evenings, I'll stand at the grill in the backyard of my house. I'll flip burgers as Jacob and Ali and their friends splash in our pool and warm Memphis light filters through the trees.

Maybe once in a while, someone will visit—Carlos or Landon or Romelu or Mulch. We'll talk about the good old days. We'll distill all those years into a highlight reel. We'll remember the glorious last-minute kicks, the laughter and clowning around in the locker room, those magnificent pileups after we'd created—at least for a fleeting moment in time—a kind of magic.

As we reminisce, we'll forget all about those long

waits in airports, the plane rides and bus rides, the bruised muscles and fears of injury, the stomach-churning anticipation of games. And all those nights I spent lying in hotel rooms, yearning for two tiny hearts that were beating away on a different continent. Those things will be long forgotten.

Maybe the kids will tease us gently as we talk, dismissing us as old men talking about bygone days.

Then maybe we'll all go inside and catch a game on television. We'll sit around and cheer for whoever's playing.

Anyone, that is, but Liverpool or Mexico.

If that's all my future holds, it will be enough.

The future doesn't seem as far away as it once did. I can see it moving toward me now, can feel myself stretching toward it.

If I reach long enough, with enough conviction, I'll secure it at exactly the right moment.

I'll know it's safe.

But for the moment, I take a few steps back and forth in goal. I feel the turf beneath my cleats. I look out to the stands, then back to center field. There, a team in bright blue and a team in red take their positions. Romelu's in front of me. Leon Osman. All those good Everton guys in blue.

Deflection – when the ball bounces off a player.

Draw – a tie at the end of a game, where neither team wins.

Ejection – a disqualification or dismissal of a player.

Equalizer – when a player scores a goal to tie the game.

FIFA (**Fédération Internationale de Football Association**) – the official soccer organization for the world.

Free kick – a direct or indirect kick on goal taken from the spot a fouled player is in or where a violation occurs when the referee stops play.

Friendly game – a game between national teams or club teams that is played outside of an international tournament or league cup competition.

Fullback – a defensive player.

Goal area – the six-yard box surrounding the goal on the field.

Goalkeeper (or keeper) – the player on the team whose job it is to defend the goal from any shots getting in.

Injury time – added time to the game after each half to make up for interruptions such as injuries and substitutions.

Knockout stage – when teams are knocked out of a tournament in which at least four teams are participating, after not winning a certain amount of games.

National team – an all-star team that represents a country.

Parry – when the keeper blocks a shot on goal but does not hold on to the ball after.

Penalty kick (PK) – a shot taken on goal from the penalty spot when a foul or a violation occurs within the box; only the keeper is allowed to defend the shot.

Red card – a player is shown a red card after being shown two yellow cards or if a dangerous or illegal play has been committed; the player is then taken out of the game and cannot be replaced.

Regulation time – the two completed periods of a game before going into overtime or extra time.

Shoot-out – a way of resolving a tie after overtime in a game.

Shutout – a game where the opposing team doesn't score a goal.

Striker – a player who primarily plays offense and tries to score against the opposing team.

Wall – a line of players protecting the goal from a free kick by the opposing team.

Winger – a player who primarily plays attack.

World Cup – an international soccer tournament that takes place every four years in which qualifying national teams play. The winning team is considered the world's best.

Yellow card – a player is shown a yellow card as a warning against certain offenses committed during a game.

ACKNOWLEDGMENTS

WRITING A BOOK REQUIRES, BY NECESSITY, SELECTING JUST a few stories while leaving others untold. My life has been filled with remarkable people, with whom I've shared extraordinary moments. I wish I could include all in these pages. If you've been a part of my life—if you've been among those who supported me and laughed with me and rooted for me—please know that you're in my heart, even if you're not in these pages.

I am the player I am because of the teammates I've had, both past and present. To my teammates on Everton and the US National Team: You are my brothers, my fellow comrades, my friends. Thank you for giving me more incredible memories than one man deserves in his lifetime. Thank you, too, to my teammates on the Metro-Stars, the Imperials, and to all my youth and school teams . . . right down to the North Brunswick Recreation Rangers. My experiences with all of you helped shape me.

To fans of US Soccer and Everton: you are the twelfth man on that field, and we'd be nothing without you. Special thanks, too, to the American Outlaws, who helped America discover the beauty and thrill of this game. I really do believe that we will win.

To the entire Everton staff: you have truly become my family. Special thanks to Sue Palmer, Bill Ellaby, Paula Smith, David Harrison, Tony Sage, Danny Donachie, Darren Griffiths, Jimmy Comer, Richie Porter, Matt Connery, Robert Elstone, and Jimmy Martin. I'll bleed blue for the rest of my life. And most of all to Bill Kenwright: your faith in me continues to be an honor.

It's been a privilege to represent my country on the world stage. I'm grateful to US Soccer for giving me the opportunity and for helping this New Jersey kid's dreams come true. I'd like to offer a special debt of gratitude to Dan Perkins, Michael Kammarman, Ivan Pierra, Dr. George Chiampas, Jon Fleishman, Jesse Bignami, and Andreas Herzog. Also, Sunil Gulati, Dan Flynn, and Don Garber, and so many others at MLS and US Soccer who work every day toward taking American soccer to new heights.

To Dan Segal, the most humble, practical, hardworking guy I know. You've had my back in this book, just as you have everywhere else. To Daren Flitcroft and Allison Brill, for your thoughtful, careful review and insights.

To my assistant, Amber: without your hard work and

dedication, my life would descend into chaos. Thank you, sincerely, for saving me from that fate.

To Mulch: it is fair to say that this book, and indeed my whole life, would be very different—and far less— without you. You've been a coach, a mentor, and a dear friend. You are with me every time I take my place in the box. Here's to the 732.

To my many coaches: Bruce Arena, Bob Bradley, Alex Ferguson, Jürgen Klinsmann, David Moyes, Roberto Martínez, and my goalkeeping coaches, Peter Mellor, Inaki Bergara, and Chris Woods. Thank you for trusting me and for pushing me.

To my editor, Nancy Inteli, for her very thoughtful and thorough attention on an astonishingly tight deadline. And to Nicole Hoff and the entire HarperCollins team: for your calm, steady guidance on such a narrow timeline.

To Ali Benjamin, who worked tremendously hard on very tight deadlines, accommodated my crazy schedule, and yet remained steadfastly committed to my cause. She spent hours and hours collecting my various thoughts, ideas, and stories and turned them into a book that I am proud to share with the world.

To NBC Sports, which has given me the honor of broadcasting Premier League games, and to my commercial sponsors, past and present, who support me and also support the sport of soccer. Special mention goes to my long-standing partner, Nike, who helped make me a pro in the first place with the Project-40 program and has been with me my whole career.

To the million or so other people who helped shape my story: Chris Brienza, Rob Skead, Ross Paule, Clint Mathis, Rob Vartughian, Steve Senior, Ed Breheny, Stan Williston, James Martin, and Reverend Hooper. I'm so honored to have shared time with you. And to the admirable people I've met through the TS community: Faith and Kim Rice, Marisa Lenger, the Kowalski family, and everyone at the New Jersey Center for Tourette Syndrome and the Tourette Syndrome Association: thanks for sharing your stories and for helping change the world.

I'm endlessly grateful to my family. To my father: thank you for your love and support.

To Chris: you're the warrior, my brother.

To my grandparents—Poppa, Momma, and Nana. I love you, and I know I'll see you all again one day.

To my mom—my rock, my inspiration, my unconditional support.

To Laura. I'm so grateful to you, both for who we once were and for who we still are today. We made two miracles. If I scoured the whole world, I could never find a better mother for Jacob and Alivia.

And, finally, to my beautiful children: my blessings, my heartbeats. Everything has been for you. Always.